EMPTY CALORIES AND MALE CURIOSITY

STORIES

TED MCLOOF

cosmorama

This is a work of fiction. Names, characters, places, and incidents either are the product of the author's imagination or are used fictitiously. Any resemblance to actual persons, living or dead, events, or locales is entirely coincidental.

Copyright © 2025 by Ted McLoof

All rights reserved. No part of this book may be reproduced or used in any manner without written permission of the copyright owner except for the use of quotations in a book review. For more information, address: hmryan@cosmorama.site.

First paperback edition December 2025

Edited by H.M. Ryan

Cover design by Lizzie Freilich

Interior design by H.M. Ryan

ISBN 979-8-9870401-4-0 (paperback)

ISBN 979-8-9870401-5-7 (ebook)

www.tedmcloof.com

cosmorama.site

PRAISE FOR TED MCLOOF

"Askew humor. Descriptive twists. The ability to touch a soul in its depth. Emily Dickinson advised writers to 'tell it slant,' but Ted McLoof tells it in all sort of directions: slant, upside down, twirling around. You never quite know where his stories are going. That's a good thing. Life as surprise. As paradox. As puzzle. I'm still thinking about these stories."

— GRANT FAULKNER, AUTHOR OF *THE ART OF BREVITY* AND CO-FOUNDER OF MEMOIR NATION

"McLoof's latest collection offers refreshing turns on the complexity of coming of age. These stories refrain from romanticizing the highs and lows of an anxious time of life and captivate us with honest, winning characterizations—of the young people we all once were and maybe even the adults we feared becoming. Witty, nostalgic, and brightly charged."

— MANUEL MUÑOZ, AUTHOR OF *THE CONSEQUENCES*

"These linked stories trace a boy's coming of age in a small New Jersey town after the rupture of his parents' marriage, a specter that haunts the rest of the book. Movies, an obsession the protagonist inherited from both his parents, become his compass. He maps his parents' relationship with Tom Cruise roles. As he says of a friendship, "Our entire language was movie quotes. Ted McLoof is a quietly devastating writer. These stories ache with adolescent longing. They're funny, companionable, and best of all, genuine. No bs here."

— MICHELLE ROSS, AUTHOR OF *THEY KEPT RUNNING*

"The casual brilliance of Ted McLoof's fiction has always astonished me. Imagine an unassumingly bookish-looking guy walking into a rowdy bar, taking off his glasses, and kicking everyone's ass at pool without breaking a sweat: This is how McLoof writes. In his stories, young people bumble their way through high school, dead-end jobs, and ramshackle nights smoking pot in cars, but before you know it, what initially felt intimate has grown large enough to contain stunning truths about the world. Honest, hilarious, and heartbreaking, McLoof's fiction may kick your ass at pool, but it'll buy you a drink afterward, and it'll be your friend forever."

— BEN RYBECK, BOOKSELLER AND AUTHOR OF *HOUSATONIC*

For my parents, who treated us way better than any of the parents in this book, and for my sisters, who can confirm.

"All I'm saying is that if I ever start referring to these as the best years of my life, remind me to kill myself."

Randall 'Pink' Floyd, *Dazed and Confused*

CONTENTS

Acknowledgments   xi

Forever Town   1
Cicadas   11
The Goddam King of the American Dream   23
The Freaks Who Suspect They Could Never
Love Anyone   40
Elegy for a Sporting Goods Store   56
Future Girl   66
The View from Hawthorne Heights   83
Rumspringa   95
If I Call You Uncouth   106

Publication Credits   117
About the Author   119

ACKNOWLEDGMENTS

First and foremost, thank you to my wife and partner in crime Sydney, whose introduction into my life kickstarted a renewed creativity that led to this collection.

Thanks to Ben Rybeck, who liked a couple of my coming-of-age stories and said, "Why don't you write a few more and make it a collection?"

To Oliver Kammeyer and Melissa 'Gutz' Gutierrez, who patiently read every single one of these pieces before anyone else did, gave tough love to the ones that needed it, encouraged the ones that were ready. This book would not exist without you.

To Jeremy and Melissa, who have zero obligation to read any of what I write but always put aside time to read it before I send it out anywhere for publication, and who are the only two people on earth who quote pop culture more than the characters in this book.

To my beloved dog Honey, who kept me company while I wrote at home and refused to let me work for more than twenty minutes at a time.

To Danny and Paul at Espresso Art Cafe, thanks for giving me a place to sit and write most of this.

Appropriately, for Mrs. Wecht, my high school creative writing teacher, the only teacher at MPHS who ever seemed happy to see me and said, Keep doing what you're doing.

FOREVER TOWN

On June 7th, 2023, Jay Levin of the *New York Times* posted an article titled "Midland Park, N.J.: A 'Forever Town' Where You 'Buy a House and Stay.'" It was supposed to be complimentary—you know, one of those *Times* profiles persuading people to buy property there, where they interview more area realtors than actual residents—but even the herculean efforts of real estate hagiography had trouble pitching our town. You almost feel bad for Levin catching this assignment. To disguise Midland Park's shoebox size, Levin uses journalistic euphemisms like "rich with the trappings of small-town suburbia." He points out that the local Dunkin' Donuts moving from one location on Prospect Street to another location on Prospect Street qualifies as "big news." He does what he can with the fact that the highlights are a mill, a train station, and a hot dog stand. He doesn't really know what to do with statistics like nine churches within 1.5 square miles, or the lowest income level in the otherwise wealthy county, or that, being of the lowest income, we had one of the highest per-capita death tolls in the Vietnam

War. He interviews residents who reflect this blue-collar-dom, an elementary school teacher and a utility worker and a hairdresser and a sewage plant supervisor, the last of whom opines that small towns are great, except that "everyone knows your business." He notes that because of the low cost and no-one-gives-a-shit-about-it-otherwise nature of the place, it was "discovered" during the pandemic, which is pretty rich since it'd been around for more than a century by then.

Despite this unflattering profile, everyone I grew up with shared the link on Facebook within hours of its publication. Someone finally acknowledged our town. And not just someone: the *New York* fucking *Times!* Who cares what it said? We were getting our moment in the sun, our fifteen minutes, or seconds, or milliseconds, whatever. No such thing as bad press.

I guess. I had a hard time with it, if I'm honest. I wonder if any of the others who shared the link had to put reservations aside to muster up the requisite enthusiasm. Anyone who grew up there must have, like me, heard echoes of themselves at the mention of the houses' many "teenage hangout basements commandeered" by the town's bored and horny sons and daughters. Anyone who grew up there must have heard something ominous in what one realtor bafflingly thinks is a glowing sales pitch: "a forever town where people buy a house and stay."

~

MIDLAND PARK'S Centennial took place in 1994. I wasn't quite eleven. The mayor planned twelve celebrations, one per month. Live library readings of books on local history in January, a public drop box where residents left 'Valentines to the Town' in February, full-costumed reenactments of Johnny Vander Meer's back-to-back no-hitters in March, a meet-and-greet with the town's Veterans on Memorial Day. That kind of thing. It was exactly what you're picturing.

But in June, they went all out. The kids were out of school, the weather warm, and it was time for the showstoppers. Mayor Faith Walker commissioned a full-on Midland Park Day Carnival in the field behind the high school, put on by volunteer residents, culminating in a variety show at night in the school's auditorium. My friends' parents manned booths together, moms took tickets and dads handed out ping-pong balls to toss into goldfish bowls. The town was a hundred years old and my parents had been married for twenty, but lately they slept in different rooms —Dad in their bedroom, Mom in a sleeping bag on my floor. So it wasn't unusual that when I found Dad at the carnival, he was by himself, in a period-accurate 1894 swimsuit, ready for the Dunk Tank. "Hey, buddy," he said. A crowd of kids gathered and I could see he'd drawn the short straw.

"Where's Mom?"

"Your mother," he said—this was another quirk, in addition to the separate bedrooms, they'd adopted in the past year, "is probably at rehearsal. She'll be there all day if you need anything." Mom was a theater director, and in fact had ambitiously created two separate theater companies when they moved here. Profits went to scholarships for graduates of the high school, so on days like this, the municipality solicited her to pitch in and do pretty much whatever she wanted.

I decided to change the subject. "Hey," I said, looking around at the carnival. "1952."

This was a game we played. He smiled, getting it. "*The*

Greatest Show on Earth." I handed him a towel. He looked around at the citizens of Midland Park and said, "1980."

"*Ordinary People.* Too easy."

"Listen, I gotta get up on that seat. Best Pictures'll have to wait."

"Okay," I said. "You'll be here all day?"

He looked at the towel and realized it would be dumb to hold it on the dunk chair. "All morning. I have the first shift," he sighed, and tossed it to me. "But I'll be useless to you while I'm up there. Do me a favor. That water's cold as a witch's tit. Tell your friends to take it easy on me."

He nodded at the crowd when he said 'friends,' but I couldn't spot any. They were older kids—high school mostly, but some from my class, the meatheads-in-training who played Smear the Queer at recess and spat on the pavement whenever a few seconds passed without an arm to punch, like a reflex. The chance to jerk themselves off over how hard they could throw, in front of a crowd, and be rewarded by immersing an adult in ice water? They were practically frothing.

MY MOTHER WAS, indeed, in the auditorium when I got there. The houselights were off and she sat in the last row, her usual technique (*make them project!*). Onstage, a group of septuagenarians called the Happy Tappers from the old people's home on Godwin Ave performed the Charleston to a song from *Thoroughly Modern Millie.* Mom's show was ten numbers through time, one for each decade of Midland Park's existence. They were in the Roaring Twenties now.

When they were done, I asked, "Are you rehearsing in order?"

She jumped a bit—I don't think noticed me in the dark next to her or heard me come in over the music but smiled when she saw me. "Hey honey," she said. "What do you mean—*Take five minutes! Bob, set it back up from the top!*—what do you mean in order?"

I looked at the stage, where wrinkly arms and legs flailed from flapper dresses, and pointed. "This is the '20's, right? Did you skip over our part?"

Mom had written an original skit for the 1910's: a live-action re-enactment of a silent film starring her, Dad, and me. In it, they'd be a couple-about-town, and I'd be a pickpocket in a newsboy cap. I'd steal Dad's wallet, they'd chase me, then catch me and take my pocket watch and I'd chase them. The kicker was that we'd perform it in front of a strobe light to give it the verisimilitude of the flickering frames of the silent film era. Mom showed me in our living room one night with the lights off. It looked amazing.

But she'd come up with the concept a year before, when Mayor Walker first commissioned the projects, and in that time the three of us hadn't practiced together once, rarely found ourselves in the same room. Mom promised we'd finalize it the day of, at dress rehearsal. I was getting nervous. She didn't seem bothered. "We're just rehearsing whoever's ready. Don't worry, kiddo."

"Are we gonna do ours though?"

"Your father," there it was again, "will be busy at the booths all day. Just practice your part on your own if you're nervous, you'll be fine."

"Aren't actors supposed to rehearse together?"

"They practice dialogue. You don't have any lines to memorize. It's a silent film. I think you're safe." She turned back to the stage, where the Happy Tappers were lined up again. The pit killed time by practicing their 40's number, "Boogie Woogie Bugle Boy." "Alright everyone, places!"

I walked away repeating her last words to me in my head, *you're safe, you're safe, you're safe.*

MAYBE IT WAS the dramatists in all of us, but our family had managed entrances and exits from any given room of the house, even the house itself, over the past year with precision timing, such that none of us were ever in the same place at once. My older sister, a high school senior, spent a lot of time at her boyfriend's house, and now that it was summer had one eye on the Rutgers campus she'd inhabit in a few weeks. Dad travelled a lot for business, I couldn't tell you where. Mom was one of those community mothers who collected committees to lead, volunteer opportunities to partake in, PTA causes to take up. I just pinballed, *Mom-Dad-Emily, Dad-Emily-Mom,* colliding with all three of them without ever attaching to any.

Mom and Dad kept all this to themselves—or Mom did; Dad just absented himself from small-town gossip altogether—so no one knew. Tonight would be the first time the three of us would be together, in front of more or less the whole town, and I didn't trust my own talent for disguising the rift. So I took Mom's advice and practiced out in the hallway. I had a feeling she was telling me to rehearse more than just the choreography of the chase.

The trick of the chase was that we couldn't actually run. The strobe light was stationary, so the blocking meant we needed to remain downstage right, where it was mounted, and run in place, creating only the *effect* of a chase. We would always be roughly a foot out of reach of each other. I worked for at least an hour in the hallway, Running Manning my way to a cartoon foot race. Rick Derris, a jock from the grade above me, and some kid I didn't know rounded the corner to get Gatorades from the vending machine. They caught me mid-slow-motion-running-in-place and didn't say anything to me, but I heard Rick mutter *fag* under his breath as they walked away.

I searched my way back through the carnival to find my dad or sister or anyone I knew from class. The town couldn't afford Ferris wheels or tilt-a-whirls or rides of any kind really, but DIY attractions covered the field anyway: Ed Harmon brought his son's BB gun and a paper bullseye for people to shoot; Principal Freeman showed off his hitherto unknown juggling skills; Carol Ann Mejury—our lunch lady—guessed people's weights and her husband, Jim, had even built a high striker from scratch for people to test their strength on, complete with mallet and bell. There was even a barbershop quartet, led by Chief Monarch and three other officers.

When I found Dad, he was pissed. There was a vulnerability in the tank no one had accounted for, a kill switch that collapsed the seat the dunkee sits on. Little assholes snuck back there all day, Dad getting dunked without notice, which put him on edge. But at least his shift was over.

"Wanna rehearse?" I asked. "If you're cold, the running might warm you up."

He patted himself down with the towel, still looked over his shoulders for punks who might jump him. The paranoia distracted him. "Running?"

"Yeah. You're supposed to chase me, remember?" That he didn't seem to have any idea what I meant did little for my confidence.

"Right," he said. "Maybe in a bit. Right now I gotta get

out of this wet bathing suit as fast as I can. I got icicles hanging off my testicles."

"Iceticles," I said, and he laughed.

"Find your sister. I saw her by the baseball diamond. The bleachers. There, where I'm pointing."

EMILY WASN'T under the bleachers. Instead, she and her friends stood on the patch of grass behind the snack bar. It wasn't quite the designated smoking area, but it may as well have been, the spot on school grounds where no teachers would bother you, sometimes smoke *with* you, at lunch.

"What the hell are we even celebrating?" I heard her boyfriend, Sean, say.

"I don't know what everyone else is celebrating," Emily said, "but I'm celebrating getting out of here. Just pretend it's one big bon voyage party for us and it's way less depressing."

Steve Spinelli, the varsity pitcher, didn't look convinced —even at ten I could tell he was bummed to graduate away from a town that worshipped him. It didn't occur to me that he was also stoned. But then he saw me and said, "Hey little man. Emily, isn't that your brother?"

She threw her cigarette down when she saw me and said, "Smoking kills," and they all laughed. "What are you doing back here?"

"Dad said to find you," I told her.

She rolled her eyes. "Fuck. Why? Did he see me smoking back here?"

"Just blame it on me," Sean told her, but she dug around in her purse for some Altoids anyway.

"Don't worry," I said. "I think he was just trying to get me to quit bugging him. Mom too." I looked at Sean and then

Steve and then Sean and then Steve and then Emily, unsure if I'd sound lame admitting this in front of them, but she nodded at me, like, *just say it*, and all my nerves about how they'd do in tonight's performance pushed me to comply: "I'm worried about them."

Before Emily could respond, Steve looked at me with bloodshot eyes and said, "Hey man, it's not the end of the world. My folks split up last year and all that changed is twice the birthday presents."

I thought Emily might kill him. I've never seen her look at anyone the way she looked at Steve Spinelli that afternoon. She didn't have to say anything for him to offer, "Fuck. My bad."

Emily turned from all three of us, looked East at the New York City skyline, then West at the sun setting behind the high school, and said, to it instead of me, "Play's gonna start soon. Go find Mom and get changed. I'll be in the front row, clapping the loudest."

IT'S NOT like I hadn't seen it coming, to whatever degree that's possible. But even so, the air felt different backstage, standing between the two of them, knowing this thing they hadn't told me yet. It frightened me how quickly and easily I could picture them as a divorced couple, as strangers, as a couple of people who used to date and were married for a bit and hey, even had a kid or two, but otherwise didn't know each other. I could picture it even at that moment, as she fixed his tie, this intimate gesture suddenly meaningless between these two people.

She moved to me next and tucked my shirt in where I'd missed a spot, fidgeted with my newsboy cap. I studied her face for signs I hadn't noticed before Steve's beanspilling: nothing. Both of them: Uta Hagen-like facial control, Stanislavskian method performances. If one of the three of us would expose things to the town during the skit, I realized, it would be me.

As Mom fixed my costume, Dad nodded to the actors onstage singing "I Remember it Well" from *Gigi* and said, "1928."

"*Broadway Melody*," I told him, instinctively, even though *Gigi* itself had won Best Picture in 1958 and felt more relevant. I wish I'd had the frame of mind to say 1979—*Kramer vs. Kramer*—but I didn't, and anyway it would have been too on the nose.

We heard the applause, held hands, and got ready to step into the strobe light.

IN THE END, it went fine. No one in the crowd suspected anything—I mean, of course they didn't, what possible fuckup could I have committed that would have given away my parents' impending divorce? The performance went okay, too. Mom was right: if you aren't talking, being together doesn't matter. They pantomimed shopping, I snagged a wallet from Dad's back pocket, the strobe light winked at us as they ran in place for the effect of a long chase. The town applauded as they caught me. The town laughed as I pivoted and ran after them, my parents, as I ran in place behind them, reached my hand out for them, both just out of my grasp.

CICADAS

I remember the night Alex Irby knocked on my bedroom window. It was the summer of '99 and I was fifteen. The cicadas were leaving their husks everywhere and wouldn't shut up. My father had moved out the year before and we couldn't afford the house anymore, so when Alex Irby peeked through my window with her hand to her forehead, I imagine all she saw was a bunch of cardboard boxes and me asleep on a sheet on the floor.

"Hey," she said, and tapped her fingernails, *1-2-3-4-5-1-2-3-4-5,* on the pane to wake me up.

"Shit," I said, but I didn't shout it (*Shit!*); I just said it like I was saying *hi*. I don't think I registered that this was real right away. I'd spent so many nights imagining scenarios involving Alex Irby just like this one—in fact, I'd jerked off to her yearbook picture just before falling asleep that very night—that it seemed impossible that she was actually there, right now, in a zip up hoodie and track shorts the forest green of our school's logo.

I stumbled in the dark and opened the window.

She looked at me blankly for a second, like she'd been looking for another dude and just realized she'd gotten the house wrong. But then she smiled her big lab-partnery smile at me. "Come on."

"Huh?"

"Let's hang out."

"What time is it even? What the fuck?"

"It's like 10:30. What are you, 300 years old?"

I poked my head out the window and saw her knees getting red as she knelt on the tar-and sandpaper of my roof. "How'd you get up here?"

"I levitated."

"Teach me?"

"If you cover up that little wiener of yours and get out here."

I shoved a reflexive hand in front of the gaping hole of my fly and almost went hard at the thought that Alex Irby had just referred to my penis, that she'd seen it, that a second ago there was nothing between my penis and Alex Irby but the July humidity.

She lit a cigarette while I pulled my own Panthers cross-country shorts on, and when she saw them she said, "We match!" and handed me a cigarette of my own.

"My mom's a bitch," Alex Irby said when I asked her why she came over.

"Your mom's a bitch so you walked all the way to my house?"

"It's two blocks, don't flatter yourself."

We were walking on my lawn and the cherries from our cigarettes looked at home with the fireflies.

"I'm just saying," I said, "I don't get why you came here;" by which I meant *me me me me me why are you here to see me tell me what's so special about me me me me me*—

"I think she wanted me to be a boy," she said, and I didn't get it.

"I don't know what that means."

She shrugged and took another puff of her cigarette as if the sentence didn't need any further explanation. "I don't mean, like, she tried to make me one. Like I was a boy and then changed or something. But I think she wanted one."

"Why do you think that," I said, because Alex Irby seemed so clearly the definition of what a girl was and what a girl is supposed to be that I couldn't imagine anyone ever wanting otherwise.

"Because she tells me," she said. "All the time." And then she squinted and pointed at me with her cigarette and put on that voice everyone used to imitate parents: "You were supposed to be a boy!"

"My mom," I said, and looked up at her bedroom window. The light was off but I knew that didn't mean she was asleep. But before I could finish the sentence Alex Irby pointed to the fenced-in pool area. "Hey," she said. "Let's swim," and I said, "In what."

She kicked off her flip-flops and unzipped her hoodie and I glimpsed the white Nike swoosh on her sports bra. It felt like someone took off my head and threw up in my brain. "In this," she said.

BUT WHEN I had asked what we were gonna swim in, that's not what I'd meant. Mom couldn't afford to service the pool since Dad left, so what used to be the neighborhood hotspot–a place we'd invite the families on the street to cool off and barbecue and play Marco Polo and time laps and practice diving and learn the breast stroke–that community pool in my backyard had turned into what Alex Irby and I were looking at now: an Olympic-sized cement hole in the ground.

"What the fuck," she said, looking at the pool rather than me. "I know," I said and she went, "Gatsby, these are some seriously questionable conditions you're living under," and I told her, "Yeah that's not news." I looked at the pool too and then closed my eyes, tried to will it full of lukewarm, chlorinated sex water. I would have given anything to skinny dip with Alex Irby and it felt like a particularly nasty O. Henrian joke that all the ingredients for that were here except the most important one. Just when I was about to open my eyes and apologize to her, my wish came true for the second time that night: I heard water splashing onto the pavement like a bathtub faucet. I opened them to see that resourceful Alex Irby had dropped our garden hose into the pool.

"Are you kidding? It's freezing," I said, with the words *little wiener* echoing in my head now.

"It's like ninety degrees out."

"It's loud, you'll wake my mom up."

She took her unzipped hoodie off completely now and said, "Do you want to do this or not?" Alex Irby was captain of the debate team and it wasn't hard to see why.

ALEX IRBY WAS the most confusing girl I knew at a time in my life when every girl was confusing. They'd write you a note with I's dotted with hearts during algebra and by lunch they'd be making out with Rick Derris. But the other girls were never confusing about who they *were*, just who they were to *you*. Alex Irby was friends with everyone. She was on the cross-country team and in the plays. She ran Dayna Caine's campaign for class president and ditched school after lunch on Fridays to get stoned. She wore berets in her hair and Nike Shox on her feet. She had a divorcee's posture and a college-girl's J. Crew sweaters and braces on her teeth. She went to almost every party but you could always find her, by the end of the night, by herself in someone's front yard looking at the sky, or wandering toward the school playground to swing on the swings alone, or talking intensely to whoever had showed up without a friend.

Who knew what was going on in Alex Irby's brain?

I would have killed for that kind of mystery. Where Alex Irby was a walking question mark, I was a five-foot-two exclamation point. It was a small shitty school in a small shitty town where everyone knew everyone else's shit, so when Dad left everyone knew he took his money with him and the lunchladies, all friends of my mom, had started sliding me free food in the cafeteria.

"Jesus," Alex Irby was saying now. "Cold."

"I told you!"

She was sticking her toe in the water. We'd only filled it two feet deep by five feet wide. She looked at me with her arms across her chest, hugging herself, daring me with her eyes to go first.

"What's that sound," she asked. I listened for my mom for a terrifying second before I realized what she meant. "The cicadas?" and she said "I guess," and I said, "Have you not heard them all summer? They live underground their whole lives. They only come out every seventeen years."

And for the first time I'd ever seen, Alex Irby looked

deflated. Like she'd been slapped. "That's the saddest thing I've ever heard," she said.

I REACHED out my leg and nudged her closer to the water with my foot.

"You better not, asshole."

I didn't know whether to blush or laugh and so I just sat down. It was weird. The flood light that normally lit the pool underwater was shining directly at us like a spotlight from behind, and it made two elongated shadows on the aqua paint. The paint was peeling in curlicues from being exposed all summer in the dry heat. Every now and then one would flake off and lightly echo when it hit the pool's vinyl floor. She sat down next to me and pulled out another cigarette and there was something in her mood that had changed.

"So what's with your mom," I asked.

She scrunched her face like she'd forgotten she had a mom until I'd reminded her. "What's with yours," she asked.

"Mine's crazy," I said. She was the first person I'd ever told that to. "But I'm not the one sneaking out in the middle of the night to get away from her."

"Jesus, Gatsby," she said. "You're so dramatic."

"Why do you call me that?"

"Gatsby?:

"Yeah."

She shrugged. "Because you're so dramatic."

She handed me a cigarette and before I could ask for her lighter, she lit it with the cherry on hers, leaned in to my face so that the ends could kiss. Then she blew out her response with the smoke. "You ever think about parents?"

"I don't know what that means."

She tapped ash off her cigarette.

"I mean, what they did when they were this old? What they were like? I can't stop thinking about that. Like, where were they the last time the cicadas were here?"

"Give me an example," I said, not because I wasn't catching on but because I'd been thinking something similar lately. We were looking at each other's shadows in front of us as we talked.

"Mrs. O'Neill ," she said, talking about Ben and Ashley O'Neill's mom. "The cops in town stop by her house while Mr. O'Neill is at work, right? And she's clearly fucking, like, half the officers."

I'd seen the cars. I knew what she meant. I just never heard anyone say it so casually before. "Maybe she's not," I said.

She either didn't hear me or didn't care. "But why? What was going on in her house, when she was our age, that makes her ok with that? And do the cops all know about each other? Do they talk about it? Did they do this shit when they were younger—like did they learn it?"

"Maybe," I said. "Or maybe they're the guys who never got laid and they're making up for lost time."

"Or trying to prove something," she said and I said, "Or maybe they really like her. I've talked to Mrs. O'Neill before. She's nice. Maybe she listens to them, or maybe she's lonely."

"But that's my point," said Alex Irby as she flicked her cigarette away. "She wasn't *born* lonely, was she? Nobody comes out of the *womb* like that. So did someone or something do that to her? Or is it just like this inevitable thing that happens to people?"

I got up and felt the water again, a little warmer from the

summer air. Without looking back at her I said, "OK—here's one. Do you think your parents talked about how to be your parents?"

"You mean like birth control?" she said. She walked to the opposite side of our little puddle and slid her feet in. The water reflecting on the giant blue walls around us made it look like an aquarium where we were the exhibit.

"Gross. No. I mean I've been thinking about—let's say your kid wants to like, I don't know. Play *Magic: the Gathering* or something."

"That fucking card game with the wizards and stuff?"

"I mean—exactly. You know that girls his age are gonna react like that and you know it's gonna be miserable for him. So do you just say, You do you, kid? Or do you tell him to conform a little?"

"Maybe this sounds shitty," she said, "but I feel like I'd rather have my kid be cool and repressed than friendless and true to himself."

"But that's what I'm asking. That's *your* instinct. But do you think our parents talked about stuff like that? Do you think they had a plan for all that stuff? Because the thing you're talking about—What do you do when your kid starts changing into someone you don't know?"

She tapped her nails on the pool's bottom just as she had on my window, *one-two-three-four-five* etc, and they echoed like batwings in a cave. Then she kicked her foot and splashed me. I took my shirt off and slid in all the way, waiting for her to follow my lead. When she didn't, I turned over onto my stomach and pretended to be drowned.

"Hey, Gatsby," I heard her saying from under the water. I lifted my head up. "How'd your folks meet?"

"In high school," I said, though I couldn't remember them actually telling me that, since they didn't talk to or about each other. But they must have told me at some point, or else how did I know?

"You think they ever did this?" she asked.

But I didn't know what this was, whatever we were doing. For a second I forgot where I was, forgot Alex Irby was sitting a foot away from me in her underwear, forgot I was in one giant, barely-filled, spotlit objective correlative for my family's separation, forgot I was lying waist-deep in tap-warm hosewater, because Alex Irby had thrown me the question my brain had been circling like a shark fin but never figured out how to name. My mom and dad, those two people whose relationship as far as I could remember it consisted mainly of thrown china plates and screaming matches so loud that I no longer set an alarm by the time my dad moved out—no way. Nothing that starts out like this could ever end up like that, was the answer to her question. But the only thing I could say was, it turns out, the truth:

They must have.

"LET'S PLAY A GAME," said Alex Irby.

By this point we were lying on our backs on the ground, her feet facing the deep end of the pool and my feet facing the shallow, but with our faces next to each other kind of, so that strands of her wet hair were splayed out octopuslike under my head. The floodlight was hitting the water we'd splashed everywhere and the reflections that made, along with the fireflies and the cicadas and the floating cigarette cherries and the stars, made it feel like we were in something heady-but-banal, a Floyd laser light show or a disco ball at a middle school dance.

"I'll bite. What game?"

"I'll say something I've never told anyone and then you say something you've never told anyone."

I squinted at the sky. "Or else what?"

She turned her head to look at me. "Huh?"

"We tell each other stuff we haven't told other people or else what?"

"Or else nothing. You just keep doing it."

"Don't there need to be, like, stakes or consequences or something for it to be a game?"

"You're such a *boy*," she said. "That's such a *guy* thing to say." And though I was flattered to hear it (I was way more often accused of the opposite), I didn't want to piss Alex Irby off. Not now.

"OK," I said. "Go ahead. You said you'd go fir—"

"My dad hasn't been home in two months. My mom won't tell me where he went and I'm starting to think it's because she doesn't know."

I waited for her to say more. When nothing came and I looked at her, she was taking a drag of her cigarette with big eyes, waving her hand counter-clockwise in the air, and I realized she was waiting for me to take my turn.

"Oh. Um," I thought. "I'm a virgin."

"It has to be something secret."

"I've never told anyone that."

"Yeah, but it's pretty obvious."

My laugh echoed in a circle around us and then seemed to disappear into the pool's filter system "OK," I said. "My mom told me one time that she dreamed I was gone. I asked her where I went and she said 'Nowhere, you weren't anywhere, you were just gone.' She was breathing really hard."

She took another puff and said, "She shouldn't tell you

stuff like that. Then she said: "We're on welfare. My mom and grandma and me."

I said, "My mom got a job busing tables at Legends Bar downtown. It's the first job she's ever had. She cried when she got it because she doesn't want people to see her there."

She said, "My dad came home one night in the back of a cop car. It was Chief Monarch. I couldn't hear why but I saw him stumbling and my mom had to promise to put him to bed. Right away."

We were on a roll now, so I said, "Sometimes I wonder if my dad wishes he never met my mom. If he's happier now. If one weekend I'm gonna go over there to visit and he won't be there."

She chucked the butt of her cigarette out of the pool, sent it airborne with a flick of her tanned, bony wrist. Then she said, "I wonder what it was like to grow up in a big house like this."

I shrugged. I was about to tell her it was boring until I realized: "Oh—wait, was that your turn?"

She nodded and for a second I thought she was going to cry. Before I could ask why, she said, "You got to grow up like that. At least for a while."

"I—" I started, but I didn't really know how to finish. What was there to say? That your life never looks good unless it's through someone else's eyes? That everybody wants some of what everybody else has? That no one is ever happy? That Mrs. O'Neill and the police force and her parents and my parents, that all they ever needed was to just be looked after and loved a little better and maybe none of us would be in this mess now?

But I didn't know any of that yet, or didn't know how to say it anyway. So I just said, "I told you I was a virgin so that we could have sex."

"I know," she said. But neither of us moved. The cars on the street were all parked quietly in their suburban driveways, the families in the houses asleep and safe, and the only sound left in the air were the cicadas letting out their pressure-cooker hiss.

THE GODDAM KING OF THE AMERICAN DREAM

The administration hated our class. I mean: fucking *hated* our class.

"Kids," said Principal Freeman one morning, in the voice of a prison warden, "this is your substitute, Mr. MacArthur."

On the word *substitute* we took the cue from Freeman's tone, eyes alight with the nasty hunger of inmates anticipating a fresh fish.

We were surprised, when in walked not the usual harried, squirrelly societal dregs but rather a tieless, confident-looking guy in cool thrift-store tweed. He wasn't young—we'd later peg him at early forties—but he slapped Freeman on the shoulder and said, "Call me Mr. M, Bob. Please."

Freeman did something then we'd never seen him do: he blushed. "*Principal* Freeman," Freeman said back to him. Then he looked at Mr. M pitifully, as if to say *Good luck on this futile mission.*

Mr. M waited until Freeman left. "Thanks, *Bob*," he saluted the empty air where the principal had been. He took off his blazer. Rolled up his sleeves. Hopped on the desk. We waited. He waited.

Then he looked at us and, maybe in response to Freeman's last look, maybe to some warning about us he'd received earlier that day, said, "You guys don't look so scary."

MIDLAND PARK HIGH SCHOOL wasn't exactly known for its grade-A faculty. To be fair, our class was nothing to brag about, the younger siblings of more successful brothers and sisters who'd attended the school when more money'd been coming in, before No Child Left Behind had left us all behind. They saw us as burnouts and losers and rebels, actively hostile toward anyone who deigned teach us anything. It was a real chicken-and-egg situation: it wasn't clear whether we hated learning because the teachers sucked or the teachers sucked because we hated learning.

Coach Hackett spent most gym periods quizzing us about his favorite movies. Ms. Stewart kept the lights off in our classroom to stave off last night's hangover while we silently answered end-of-chapter questions in our history textbooks. The cops arrested Vice Principal Fitzgerald our junior year, we weren't sure why, though rumors said internet kiddie porn. Mr. Varjian, our math teacher, had a nervous breakdown and got in a fistfight with Jon Ragu in the middle of class. At best they were just bog-standard public school teachers, underpaid and jaded and as bored with the material as we were. Ms. Manicone, our English teacher, wasn't so bad; the worst you could say about her was that she didn't really care. Before she left we started *Death of a Salesman* and she quizzed us on things like the name of Willy Loman's best friend.

But then she went on maternity leave, and now we were looking at Mr. M, her temporary replacement, home inspectors scanning for cracks in the foundation. "OK, so: anybody not wanna read this?" he said, picking up the copy of *Salesman* on Manicone's desk.

We didn't respond. We were latchkey kids with nothing to do after school except watch TV. We knew the Cool Teacher trope and weren't going to be taken in so easily; no amount of desk-sitting or Thanks, Bob's could change that. But he was ready for it. "Tell you what," he said. "Make an argument for why we shouldn't read this, and we won't. Deal?"

Frank Bosco perked up. He was as close to a jock as you could get in a town without enough money or people for a football team. It usually took him a minute. "Seriously?" he asked.

"Yeah," Mr. M said, taking out a pack of gum and popping a piece in his mouth. "It's my first day. I don't have anything planned. You'd be doing me a favor." We looked at each other to see what was what. "Go ahead," he said. "Why shouldn't we read this?"

Gwendolyn Diaz, the aspiring flower child who'd lost her virginity at thirteen and whose mom let us stay over when we got too drunk, whispered to me, "Because it's fucking boring."

Mr. M walked over to her, leaned on her desk. "What was that?"

Anyone else would have been intimidated, but someone had to show this guy what he was up against and Gwendolyn figured it might as well be her. She straightened up, steepled her fingers mimicking an honors student and said, over-enunciating, "I said because it's fucking boring, sir."

He walked toward the board where the call button for

the principal was and Gwendolyn reached for her backpack to head to the front office. But instead of pressing it he wrote on the board

"IT'S FUCKING BORING." Now everyone went quiet. We stared at the word "fucking" in big block letters on the board, in chalk. The door to the classroom was wide open. Anyone could have walked past and seen it.

He turned to us and said, "Great. Let's keep going. Other reasons?"

Ragu raised his hand from the back row. Ragu always sat in the back row. Teachers called him the Human Thesaurus when we were kids, but now he only inhabited this persona as a party trick when we were high. Sad we'd say, and he'd say, Melancholy. Lugubrious. and we'd crack up. I couldn't remember the last time Ragu raised his hand, but he wanted to answer this question, apparently. Mr. M called on him and Ragu said, "It's *really* fucking boring?"

Mr. M smiled and said, "Sorry kiddo, no repeat answers. How about this—*why* is it so fucking boring?" Ragu hadn't accounted for this: the bravado drained from his face and he just said, "I don't know," and Mr. M said, "Yes you do, come on," and Ragu said, "I don't know," and we held our breaths —Ragu's fistfight with Mr. Varjian still fresh in our minds— but Ragu relented and said, "Because it's like fifty years old and has nothing to do with us."

Mr. M pointed his chalk directly at Ragu. "That," he said, "that—God. That's a great answer. Evidentiary support for the 'boring' answer. Kiddos, your friend there just bought us all a day." He wrote NOTHING TO DO WITH US on the board. "OK," he said. "Last question: How do you all know this thing has nothing to do with you? I've never read it. What's it about?" He waved the play around flimsily by its cover between his thumb and forefinger, like a handkerchief in a magic show or a dirty diaper, like something either very delicate or very dirty.

He looked, this time, directly at me. I felt the entire class's ability to ditch work scot-free on my shoulders here, so I attempted something—anything—Manicone told us before she left.

"Something about the American Dream or something," I said. He leaned two elbows on my desk, eye-to-eye with me, but still spoke loud enough for the class to hear. I realized when I smelled his breath that the gum he'd been chewing was Nicorette. "And what's the American Dream?" he asked. "I don't know," I told him. "She went into labor before she could tell us."

The class laughed. Mr. M did, too. "Alright," he said. "I'll take it. The American Dream is the opportunity to get whatever you want no matter how you were born. I'm not telling you anything you don't already know: this isn't a wealthy town. Your parents work hard. You're not like the rich-bitch kids in Franklin Lakes or Ridgewood," he said. Now no one was laughing. It was so true. "But I'm sure you guys want the same stuff, right? Raise your hand if you think you'll get married when you get older." Every hand went up. "OK. So why do you want to get married?"

Kara Alston, a spacey, soft-spoken girl who might as well have spoken Russian for all the times we ever heard her talk, said, "Love?"

"Is that a question?" Mr. M asked.

"Love," she repeated.

"Love's a good answer," Mr. M said. "But plenty of people fall in love without getting married. Plenty of people get married without love."

"I want to be a Band-Aid, like Penny Lane in *Almost Famous*," Gwendolyn said, her chin in her hands, leaning forward on her knees. I'd seen this look before: she was flirting with him.

"That's a great flick," he said, ignoring the look. "Bonus points for going against the status quo, Diaz," and she said, "I don't even know what 'status quo' means," and he said, "Exactly."

"Mr. M," I asked. "Not that I mind, but why the hell are we talking about this?"

"Why are we talking about this?" he wrote on the board. "Great prompt question for your homework." He picked the play up again and said, "Read some of this and tell me what the point of this conversation was."

Bosco rolled his eyes, betrayed that we were being given homework after the promise of being let off the hook. Kara Alston stared at the play on her desk, puzzled. We couldn't blame her.

"Read how much of it?" we asked. "How long should the response be?" we asked.

"Doesn't matter," he said. "You don't have to write anything. Just read it until you feel like you have an answer and then we'll talk more tomorrow."

"No written homework?" we asked. "No written homework," he said.

We loved this guy.

MY MOM TENDED bar at Legends, the townie tavern down the street from our house. After school I'd stop in and talk to her as she poured me tonic waters that I downed like the barflies I envied so much. The bar was empty as I told her about the Mr. M vs Principal Freeman smackdown.

"Well, Freeman's an asshole," she said. "Glad someone has the balls to take the piss out of him."

I nodded. Legends only had stained-glass windows, keeping the place dark, and I couldn't quite make out the look on her face. Anyway, Freeman hadn't been the point of what I'd told her, so I kept going. "Have you ever read *Death of a Salesman*?"

Mom, a former actress, scoffed at me and flipped her hair. "Read it?" she asked. "I *played* Linda Loman at Pitt in 1979!" so I asked, "Why do you think he asked us about what we wanted when we grew up? What's that got to do with the play?" and she said, "I'm not doing your homework for you," and stuck her tongue out at me. I was about to deliver some snarky comeback when I heard a familiar male voice behind me say, "Better check his ID, he looks a little young."

Mr. M patted my shoulder, sat on the adjacent barstool, ordered a whiskey Coke and a shot from Mom, who glanced at the clock glowing 4:12 and said, "Long day? Little early for shots, no?"

Mr. M hooked his jacket under the bar and said, "Celebrating, darlin'. First day on the job."

I'd heard plenty of men call my mom 'darlin' in the time she worked there, but Mr. M's tone differed—differed how, I wasn't sure yet. "Mom," I said. "This is Mr. M."

Upon hearing this she gave him an extra long pour on his whiskey Coke and shook his hand. He held her grip a beat longer than your average handshake and said, "'Mom'? You belong to this guy? The King of the American Dream over here? Only kid who knew what that meant. Must get it from mom." He winked at her and tipped back his shot.

He swiveled around on the stool like a little kid, then stopped when facing me. "What did you think of our talk today?" he asked me. "I'd love your take."

I couldn't tell what he meant—my take on the play I hadn't read? My take on the class discussion we'd cut short? I landed on the only thing I knew about: "Ragu spoke."

Mr. M laid a pack of Pall Malls, my mother's brand, on the bar. "Seems like a good kid." He was looking at Mom as she bent over for more glasses. "How come you guys don't like talking?"

I thought. "I don't think we're used to anyone asking us what we think about stuff. You wanna know the truth, I've never read a book assigned for an English class."

He lit a cigarette. "I'll let you in on a secret, pal," he said bitterly. He was already done with his whiskey Coke so he ordered another one. "No one has."

WE SPENT the next day telling everyone who'd listen about Mr. M. *He called Principal Freeman Bob*, said Bosco. *He's seen Almost Famous*, said Gwendolyn. *He liked my answer*, said Ragu. Even Kara Alston moved from wherever she usually sat at lunch to our table and said, *What do you think he meant about love?* and we traded stories of our brothers' and sisters' and parents' relationships. We realized none of us ever talked about anything—nothing important anyway, nothing personal—but now here we were, and we couldn't shut up.

The one thing we didn't talk about was *Death of a Salesman*, which by the time we entered class the next day, still none of us had read. That didn't matter though: the desks had been set up in a semicircle and Mr. M told us we'd be reading the play aloud in class, a bit of a disappointment. It was the kind of lesson we were used to from checked-out teachers who wanted an easy way to eat up minutes without actually teaching anything. When we protested this, Mr. M said, "It's a play. It's meant to be heard. Ragu, you'll be Willy Loman. Diaz, you can be Linda today."

Ragu, who'd been looking out the window at either falling snow or the sophomore girls smoking on the pitcher's mound, barely registered the directive and took a minute to find Act 1, Scene 1, page 1. When he did he read with the enthusiasm of someone reading the nutrition facts on a can of soup: "It's all right. I'm back."

Gwendolyn's flair for the theatrical helped as she read, "Willy! What happened! Slight Pause! Did something happen, Willy!" For some reason she read this in a Southern accent, her backward hand to her forehead, and Mr. M nearly spit out his coffee at the emphasis she put on "slight pause," before saying, "I'll read the stage directions, but thanks, Diaz."

The class went quiet and we waited. Whatever was outside the window had recaptured Ragu's attention and I realized he was high. "Your line, chief," Mr. M told Ragu, who looked back at the play and said, "I have to read all of this Willy guy's lines?" and Mr. M said, "You're our guy," and Ragu skimmed the pages and said, "But—he's on every page."

"Yeah, he's the protagonist, Jon. That's kind of how it works," Mr. M said, popping more of that apparently useless Nicorette in his mouth.

Ragu didn't look pleased. He cracked his knuckles. I watched him consider his options and settle on a sort of compromise: reading so ineffectively that Mr. M would regret the assignment.

"Nothing happened," he read vacantly.

"You didn't smash the car, did you?" Gwendolyn read.

"I said nothing happened, didn't you hear me?" Ragu read again, sounding genuinely pissed. I glanced at the text and noticed the stage directions for his line read with *casual irritation*, and it struck me that Mr. M had him: Willy Loman, we all discovered for the first time, was distracted, disgruntled, hollow, pissed off. He was, in other words, all of the things Ragu was in class, so his efforts to de-dramatize the role ended up embodying it. Bosco read for Happy and I caught him wince in recognition when he read, "It wouldn't be like a business, we'd be playing ball again!" We'd been tricked into becoming a living incarnation of the people Arthur Miller wrote about, and Mr. M finally asked, "OK so: what was the point of our conversation yesterday?"

I MADE it a habit of staying later at the bar than I normally would have. Each night, Mr. M grew more animated as his empty glasses stacked up, the ashtray filling with discarded butts.

"My English teacher," he said, "freshman year of high school? That guy was something else. He'd say, 'Alright everyone, this month we're reading *Long Day's Journey into Night*. I assume you've read it—don't raise your hands if you haven't, you'll embarrass yourselves.'"

I thought about that. "Sounds like kind of a dick—"

"No!" he said, banging the bartop with his fists, loudly enough that patrons looked our way. The post-work rush thickened the crowd and parents of my friends peopled the booths surrounding us. "Sorry," he said, to the TV for some reason, so I couldn't tell whether he was apologizing to me or them or both. "I just mean—there was something about that level of respect. He assumed we were at his level so we read our asses off to earn that. Does that make sense?"

My mother served Mr. Dooley, who ran Dooley's Hardware, his nightly shot at the other end of the bar, but I knew her look well: she was gaging how sauced the men in the bar were getting. If she'd had a free hand, it would have been cupped to her ear and aimed at us.

In any case, Mr. M didn't wait for an answer because he was on a roll. "*Salesman* is on Broadway now. With Brian Denehy. It's supposed to be phenomenal. Maybe I'll take you kids, make a field trip out of it."

"Can't we just watch the movie in class?" I asked. I liked him but I was a little tired of adults making promises they couldn't keep. I couldn't even conjure up an image of Frank Bosco sitting in a Broadway balcony, rapt with attention, a rolled-up Playbill in his hand.

"With Dustin *Hoffman*?" he asked, spitting the name incredulously, as though I'd suggested the primary school kids walk across the street to the high school and perform the play for us.

"Why not?" I asked. "I like Dustin Hoffman."

He took a drag and squinted, weighing the point, blew his response out with the smoke.

"Hoffman's fine when he gives a shit. But he putters around in that movie like this neurotic, nebbishy…" I could see him looking for another word besides "Jew" but in absence of it he just switched tracks. "Loman's this towering, hulking motherfucker. Because he's the embodiment of the American Dream which is also this towering hulking motherfucker, youknowwhatImean? It's all just bullshit. You're the King of the American Dream, kid, did I tell you that yet?"

He'd told me that every night since that first one so I used it as my cue to take a piss. I studied the graffitied mirror. I wasn't a towering motherfucker. I weighed about ninety pounds. When I got back his barstool held his jacket but no Mr. M. He sat now in a booth, next to two college girls laughing with or at him, it was tough to tell. "Mr. M?" I said as I approached the booth.

"*Mister* M?" one of them cackled. She pointed her cigarette at me. "Who's this?"

He held her gaze and forgot I'd even been in the bar, then glanced at me, something registered, and exploded in a smile. "This, ladies, is my wingman!" Before he could say more, Mom came with his shot on a tray and said to me, "Why don't you head on home. You've got school in the morning," and then, looking at Mr. M as she handed him his shot, said, "You both do."

THAT NIGHT, something happened: I went home and actually read *Death of a Salesman*. I wanted to get a sense of what Mr. M was always going on about. I wanted to earn this title of King of the American Dream. Mom was closing that night so, as usual, the house was empty when I fell asleep. I woke up around 3 am with the play tented on my stomach, the lights in my room still on. Our house was tiny and Mom and I shared the sole bathroom, and I realized she was home from work when I got up to pee and the bathroom was locked. I waited for the flush and didn't know what to do when the door opened and out walked Mr. M, furry chest popping out underneath his unbuttoned shirt, pinstriped, wrinkled boxers around his skinny legs, cummerbund of beer belly sagging over the waistband. I froze. He blinked at me. The cathode ray tube red-blue-green light from Mom's TV down the hall lit his profile. It reminded me of *Poltergeist*. He nodded at me, then walked down the hall, back to Mom's bedroom.

DURING THE NEXT FEW WEEKS, we ate, slept, and drank *Death of a Salesman*. We started calling Ragu 'Willy,' to his apparent delight. He even stopped getting stoned at lunch, so he could stay straight for his performances each day in English. We argued about the characters and the meaning at parties. Bosco thought Willy was a loser because he failed at being a salesman, while Gwendolyn thought Willy was a loser for actually wanting to *be* a salesman without having a reason for wanting that. Kara Alston always had the coolest takes of all of us, which we'd become anxious to hear each day. She didn't think Willy was a loser at all, thought him an idealist with the bad luck of being born in the wrong country at the wrong time, whose only mistake had been buying into what the country sold. "Oh shit," said Ragu. "So he's a failed salesman because he's buying instead of selling." "Whoa," we all said.

In class our roles became more polished. Mr. M kept the basic class structure up: twenty minutes of reading aloud, twenty minutes of talking about it. Always those open-ended questions: Are you guys any different from Willy? But why is he a loser? What do you want out of life that's any better? Is the American Dream bullshit or should we take it seriously?

But every night I found myself on that barstool next to him, my mother surveilling us peripherally. I fell asleep having imaginary conversations with him, with my mother, with him about my mother, my mother about him. I'd memorize the questions and answers of these fantasy talks and put them in my back pocket for the next night's bar-talk, except we kept following the same pattern: Mr. M and I would reassess the day's class discussion, he'd lose focus, I'd pee, he'd hit on the townie girls. On karaoke night he'd perform uninvited duets with anyone who sang Springsteen. On bar trivia night he'd slay the lit categories but argue with the MC over the categories he missed. Either he never told Mom I'd seen him in the house, or they opted to pretend it never happened. So I waited until a night when Mom wasn't working, I told her I was hanging out at Gwendolyn's, and snuck into the bar instead. I wanted to see what the night would look like without her there to cut him off, to cut us off. He spent most of the night muttering bitterly about Willy Loman. "That motherfucker Loman," he said, his head on the bar. "Daisy killed him. Daisy did him in."

"That's Gatsby," said Mr. Dooley, next to him.

"Same shit," he said into the pit of his elbow. The opening horns of "Thunder Road" drizzled out from the jukebox, notes I'd heard a hundred times before and struck me as either mournful or hopeful, I could never decide which. Mr. M looked like he was about to say something else when Gus, the bartender working the stick, interrupted us.

"Card's declined," he said, handing Mr. M his Visa.

"Run it again."

"Ran it three times, boss," he said, his hand still holding the card out to Mr. M, though he was looking at me, and for some reason I felt guilty as hell. But Mr. M stood up and said, slurring, "Not to worry, I can solve this. Where's your payphone?"

Gus pointed him toward it, he made a call while I waited anxiously, then Mr. M came back and said, "Come on, kid. Come wait outside with me for my wife."

∼

"Wife?" I asked him as we sat on the curb outside. Legends was attached to the town's 7-11 so we were aglow in the repulsive orange-green-red of the bright sign. A Yankee-capped twentysomething pulled up, blasting Biggie from his Camaro, and some kids I didn't recognize, hanging outside the door, asked him if he'd buy them cigarettes.

"Huh?" Mr. M asked, lighting one of his own.

"I didn't know you had a wife," I said.

"She's wonderful. You'll love her. Always there for me. Maybe she'll join us for a nightcap. That's important, you know, having someone who'll support you, hang in the foxhole with you."

I wasn't concentrating on his words. I was still having trouble attaching the word 'wife' with everything I knew about Mr. M, having trouble figuring out why he'd never once mentioned her, in class or at the bar or any other time. But I'd also been thinking lately, in the wake of my exposure to Willy and Linda Loman, and my mother and father's separation, that these things are more complicated than that, and maybe this—not Mr. M's words, but the fact of whatever his marriage consisted of—was another, non-literary lesson I was getting from him.

I stared at a leaky oil stain on the ground. The kids behind us had convinced the guy to buy them their ciga-rettes so I listened as they counted their change and passed Marlboros out from a pack to each other and they realized they forgot to buy a lighter as well. "I still don't get the message of *Death of a Salesman*," I said to the oil stain, for lack of anything more insightful to contribute.

His eyes were closed but he still had a lit cigarette in hand; it was hard to tell how present he was, until he said, "You kids gotta stop looking for messages."

Now I was thoroughly confused, but figured he was just

too drunk to make any sense, maybe wasn't even following the thread of our conversation. "I thought that was the whole point of reading," I said. "Jesus, you finally get us to read and now there's no message?"

"Art," he said, "shouldn't be about messages. It shouldn't give you answers to stuff you don't know. It should make you question what you think you do know. Look at Loman. Is he a hero?"

"Kind of," I said.

"Is he an asshole?"

"Kind of," I said.

"There you go," he said, but I didn't really get the thrust of his point. He still hadn't opened his eyes during all this, and kept them closed as he mumbled, "Goddam King of the American Dream." And then he threw up into the snow.

A Volvo pointed its LED headlights at us. "There she is," Mr. M messily smiled, and I was grateful he recognized his wife's car, grateful she was here to handle the mess I didn't know how to clean up. She left the engine running, and when she got out of the car, she had the expression you give a dog that shat on the carpet, a stray dog you can't remember why you'd taken in in the first place. "Get the fuck in the car," she told him. She didn't seem to notice I was there.

"Baby!" he said, wobbly arms outstretched. In lieu of taking them, she opened the passenger door and pointed. "In," she said. "You're a fucking embarrassment."

He hobbled himself to his feet, and only when he used my shoulder to hoist himself up did she notice I was with him. She handed me a wad of cash and said, "You know him?"

"He's my teacher."

"He's a drunk and a loser. Can you give this to the bar

and tell them not to serve him? I told him not to come here anymore but he won't listen to me."

I took the cash and nodded. I waved goodbye to him but he was passed out, forehead against the steamed-up window, so I just stood there with the smell of his puke wafting over me in a fog.

NONE of us got to say goodbye. Manicone returned from maternity leave the next day, without warning from anyone. We never finished reading the play aloud, and English went back to boring old English class: Manicone gave us an end-of-unit exam with questions like, "For what region is Willy responsible in his sales?"; Ragu came to class stoned again; Kara Alston stopped answering questions altogether. Mom took me to see *Death of a Salesman* on Broadway. Brian Denehy was great. For a week or two we all mourned the loss of Mr. M, laughed fondly remembering him writing "Fuck" on the board. I debated whether to tell them who he was. But they believed in him and I couldn't see the point. I couldn't get those questions out of my head: Was he a hero? Was he an asshole?

THE FREAKS WHO SUSPECT THEY COULD NEVER LOVE ANYONE

In the winter of my sophomore year, I couldn't get cocaine off my mind, but all my mom could talk about was Tom Cruise.

"I really think he has a shot this year, don't you?" my mother asked me. We were in the kitchen before school doing our usual routine: she sat at the table smoking a menthol, I cooked breakfast, which in our house meant unwrapping foil from a pair of frosted cinnamon Pop-Tarts.

"I wouldn't get my hopes up," I said, placing the Pop-Tarts in the toaster. "He's lost before."

"It's different this time," she said. She'd woken me up at 4:30 a month before for the AMPAS announcement of this year's Oscar nominees—a tradition of ours—and Cruise, her favorite actor, had been nominated for his performance in *Magnolia*. "Don't you think he'll win?"

"I don't know," I said. "I haven't seen it yet."

She blew out an incredulous puff of smoke. "Theodore, have I taught you nothing? You don't have to see it to make a prediction. You just have to follow the trades." On the word "trades" she gestured to the copy of *Entertainment Weekly* that splay open in front of her, the words in gold font on the front.

Mom had once been an aspiring actress; she starred in a string of off-off-Broadway shows in the 70's, her "Bohemian Years" she called them. Her fifteen minutes had been a movie-of-the-week Christmas special called *Our Christmas Alien*, as the matriarch of a family that found a friendly alien for the holidays. This had been in the early 80's, when in the wake of *E.T.*'s success networks basically pumped out friendly alien narratives on a conveyor belt and hers got lost in the shuffle. She'd been cast because she was pregnant with me, though, and she liked to say that I was an actor when I was still in the womb.

But, again, at that moment, all I could think about was coke. My friend Ragu had promised me he'd introduce me to it after school, show me a good first time, and I'd been anxious about it all week. I needed a distraction, so I threw Mom a bone. "Why is it different this year?"

"Huh?" she asked, skimming the pages of her magazine. The Pop-Tarts were done by now so I took them out and buttered them.

"You said it was different this time. Why's it different?"

Without looking up from the magazine, she said, like she was being interviewed by *Entertainment Weekly* itself for her predictions, "Because Cruise is the most generous leading man there is. That's why his goddam *co-stars* keep getting all the accolades," and she said co-stars like a curse word. "Cuba Gooding, Jr, Holly Hunter, Paul Newman, Mary Elizabeth *MastrantonIio*, for God's sake—Nicholson, the showy bastard!" She was on a roll now. "Dustin Hoffman? It takes nothing to do what he did. Not a thing. Without Cruise playing off of him, it's nothing. But now," she leaned toward me and pointed to the magazine, like I didn't already know this information, like she hadn't gone on this rant a hundred times before. "Now he's nominated for a *supporting* performance. That's the key. That's how he's gonna win." She put her cigarette out and smiled at me triumphantly through a bite of Pop-Tart, and I would have thought she was insane, but I knew, of course, that this wasn't just about Tom Cruise.

"DUDE, what is with your mom and Tom Cruise?" Ragu asked me at school when I mentioned it.

"I don't know," I said, but I did. "My mom and dad's first date was *TAPS*. She says they argued all night about whether he or Sean Penn would become the bigger star. And then she took my dad to opening night of every one of his films." This on its own wouldn't normally seem sufficient, but Ragu knew my dad left two years earlier, so when I asked, "Can we not talk about it?' he just shrugged.

"You still coming over today?" he asked by way of changing the subject.

"Of course," I said, but I didn't sound confident. "You're sure your parents aren't gonna come home early? Or smell it or anything?"

"Smell it?" he said incredulously, and let it go. "My stepmom's working a late shift at the hospital and my dad's on an overnight run with his truck. The place is ours."

In truth, I wasn't worried about getting caught—I was worried about taking this step into debauchery. One by one, our whole grade had been overtaken by drugs in the past year. I'd been an early drinker and often stole Mom's cigarettes. Ragu had gotten me into pot these past few weeks and I liked the hazy distance it gave me, which is why I spent less and less time with Mom lately. But there were lines I hadn't crossed yet that I felt wary of, and hard drug use was one of them. I wanted Ragu to say something like, *Come on, chicken! Are you too scared to snort a little white?* or something, but life was not an after school anti-drug commercial.

Instead he said, "I asked Mallory to come with us." Mallory Mays, he knew, was the queen of my dreams. She'd gotten caught painting the school's front walk one night, and her graffiti was so good that instead of suspending her, they asked her to paint murals all over the hallways of the school. She'd followed this directive by painting the cartoon characters of our collective childhoods—Bart Simpson, the Ninja Turtles, Smurfs, Roger Rabbit—in funky scenarios on every inch of the place. My favorite was the Muppets crossing Abbey Road in the music wing.

Ragu saw whatever idiotic look I had on at the sound of her name and said, "Meet me at the baseball field after school. Come on man, I'mma get you high today. Cause it's Friday, you ain't got no job, and you ain't got shit to do." It was a bit on the nose, but he knew I'd get the reference, because our entire language was movie quotes.

MY PARENTS HAD TRAINED me to be a film buff for as long as I could remember. Neither of them meant to do it. It's just who they were. Dad took me to my first rated R movie—*My Cousin Vinny*—not to initiate me into some sort of cinephilic club but because Mom was away that weekend and he didn't have anyone else to go with. Mom made me watch the Oscars, Globes, and Guild Awards with her every year not for educational purposes but because that's what she watched and they couldn't afford a babysitter.

"I could've worn that—I look great in lavender," she'd say as Nicole Kidman walked the red carpet, and it didn't take Freud to know she saw her own stalled film career in the glamorous actors at these shows, an alternate universe, a flip of the coin where she'd pursued her dreams to their successful ending point. Dad didn't join us for most of that —he wasn't big on awards ceremonies and he was around less and less in those years before his departure, anyway— but he always joined us for the Oscars. The last Oscars we ever watched with him had been a few years before. Cruise had been nominated that year as well, for *Jerry Maguire*, and I could still remember the look they gave each other when Geoffrey Rush beat him: a kind of loving condolence, the last look of love between them I could recall.

So when I called Mom from the school pay phone that day at lunch, I wasn't surprised that she didn't want me to go to Ragu's.

"I was going to get tickets for us to *Magnolia* tonight. It's playing at the Triplex in Hawthorne. Martha's working, she can get us free popcorn."

I looked around at the crowded hallway, hoping Ragu or, worse, Mallory wasn't in earshot. "I just—I promised Ragu I'd hang with him today."

"You've been seeing a lot of that kid lately," she said, and you could hear in her voice she knew what kind of kid Ragu was. "You hung out with him last weekend. And the weekend before. When are we gonna hang out?"

I wanted to tell her to get her own friends, but she'd lost most of them in the divorce. For a minute I considered taking her up on it as my excuse to back out of doing coke today—you know, Sorry Ragu, my mom's on my ass or whatever—but that seemed even more embarrassing than having second thoughts. "We can go another night, I promise."

"The Oscars are on Sunday. We have to see it before then."

"Tomorrow, then. Tomorrow night I'm all yours," I told her, and she said "What?" and I repeated,

"Tomorrow I'm all yours," and she said, "What?" just as Mallory passed by me, so when I shouted, "I'm all yours!" it was right in Mallory's face and she laughed so I hung up.

"What's that you have there?" I asked Mallory, meaning the piece of paper in her hand.

She seemed to have forgotten she was holding it until I pointed to it. She was a dreamy person, and often gave the impression that she'd wandered into whatever room she was in with no clue how she got there.

"Huh? Oh." She lifted it up so I could get a look. It was a sketch of Calvin and Hobbes wearing the masks of Dionysus, next to Doug Funnie in Elizabethan attire, holding Yorick's skull. "It's for the theater room," she said.

"Neat," I said, because I was an idiot and that's all I could say in the face of such artistic genius. "They just let you skip classes to paint this stuff?"

She shrugged. "Not all the time. And not every class. But I think some of my teachers are sort of over trying to teach me and the school seems to like free labor, so." With anyone else this would have been a joke, but her dry delivery kept me from knowing whether to laugh.

I couldn't think of a segue, so I just blurted out, "See you after school, I hear?"

"Maybe," she said, but she had that moony look again. It struck me she'd probably smoked a blunt before lunch, and I wondered for a moment if there was anyone left who wasn't high.

AND, in fact, she was not there when I spotted Ragu after school. Instead, Ragu stood in the dugout, smoking a Camel with Jeff Tansey. A metalhead before we knew what metalheads were, Jeff Tansey wore enormous black Jncos, a septum piercing, and painted black fingernails. Jeff Tansey was a senior, though his chances of graduating were notoriously slim since he'd mooned our math teacher Mr. Fredericks and—accidentally, he claimed—set fire to the chemistry lab.

"Where's Mal?" I asked when I approached them.

"What's the matter, asshole?" asked Jeff Tansey, flicking my sternum with his non-cigarette hand, with a force that almost knocked me over. "Disappointed to see me?" Before I could catch my breath and respond he cracked up. "I'm just kidding, kid," he said, rubbing my hair. "That chick's a cutie. I'd be disappointed to see me too."

I forced a smile and then Ragu bailed me out. "My stepmom got her shift covered, so we can't do it today. But I'm dry anyway, so Tansey's gonna hook us up with a dime."

Jeff Tansey nodded toward his car, a dented 1987 Oldsmobile, dark red rusting through its peeling paint, one rear light missing from the back. I couldn't tell what the original color was supposed to have been, but my best guess was Cookie Monster blue.

Ragu rode shotgun. The backseat was covered in fillet-o-fish wrappers and cigarette ash. The car smelled like shit if shit had been left out in the rain for three days and then sprayed with Febreeze. But I had also never ridden around in a senior's car before, and I felt like I was being inducted into the cool kids' club. Jeff Tansey blasted Pantera from the stereo at an alarmingly antisocial volume and I pretended to enjoy it by rocking my head back and forth.

When we pulled up to a house, I knew it wasn't his—we were well outside our hometown. It was a two-family split-level with a chain-link fence out front and a mattress on the browning front lawn. The house peeled paint worse than Jeff Tansey's car. The screen door lacked an actual screen, and hung on by only one hinge.

Jeff Tansey turned to Ragu and asked, "How much do you want?"

Ragu pointed his thumb at me and said, "He's buying."

This took me by surprise. I'd barely reconciled the concept of *Ragu's* coke. Now I was being thrust straight into the world of narcotics sales. I didn't even know what increments coke came in. I felt scandalized but also exhilarated and mature, even more so when Jeff Tansey, sounding genuinely impressed, looked at me and said, "Big man! Look at this guy!"

"It's his first time," Ragu told him.

"I promise I'll be gentle," Jeff Tansey said with sinister eyes, or an imitation of sinister—like Nicholson's when he faces down Tom Cruise in the courtroom of *A Few Good Men*.

"Just get me whatever this buys," I said, handing him forty bucks. His eyes widened and he said, "Jesus. You're gonna be the goddam king of the school with this." When Jeff Tansey left the car Ragu thanked me and told me we could do it at his house with Mallory on Sunday, when he knew his parents would be gone. I got quiet and he noticed, asked what was wrong.

"Sunday's the Oscars," I said. He nodded but seemed to think I was merely noting an irrelevant banality, like I'd said Sunday was the day after Saturday.

"I'll be there," I told him.

"JESUS CHRIST," Mom said as we left the theater the next night. "He was terrific. Wasn't he just terrific?" She lit a cigarette and puffed it with relish, as if it were post-coital.

"He was something else, that's for sure," I said. It wasn't that I had nothing else to say; Mom and Dad had taught me the language of film appreciation and Cruise's performance in *Magnolia* was—is—indeed a triumph. I'd spent the past two and a half hours mesmerized by Paul Thomas Anderson's never-resting manic camera lens, dizzied by the wall-to-wall soundtrack mashup of Aimee Mann and Jon Brion, caffeinated by the deliberately, gleefully over-the-top performances of Julianne Moore, William H. Macy and, above all, Tom Cruise. And it wasn't that I'd felt uncomfortable sitting next to my own mother as Cruise's character shouted, "Respect the cock and tame the cunt!" This was, after all, the same year that she'd dragged me to see *Eyes Wide Shut*, wherein Cruise participated in a ten-minute-long masked orgy.

The problem was that I still hadn't figured out how to tell her I wouldn't be watching the Oscars with her this year. Every time Melora Walters snorted coke during the movie— she did this a lot—my stomach tightened at the thought of it. Mom finished off the last of the free popcorn her friend Martha had, indeed, hooked us up with and shivered from the Jersey March night.

"Do you remember when he lost for *Jerry Maguire*? The way Nicole looked at him, that supportive little look of, 'Don't worry babe, you still have me?' He was our inside joke," she said with a sad little smile, but I knew she didn't mean me. She looked at the ground ahead of us. "In '86, when everyone involved with *The Color of Money* got nominated except Tom Cruise, I bet your father that he'd win the next one. And then in '88, when everyone involved with *Rain Man* fucking *won* except him, I bet your father again. And then in '89 when he was finally nominated—"

"—for *Born on the Fourth of July* you said double or nothing," I finished. I'd heard this stupid story so many times. It pissed me off that she talked about him like he was still around.

I guess she took my irritation as indifference because she responded, "He's only 5' 6", you know. You should be more enthusiastic about diminutive movie stars." She patted my head to emphasize how much shorter I still was than her, and I slapped it away from her, more violently than I'd meant to. "Hey," she said, her hand still patting the air where my head had just been, patting invisible me for comic effect. "What's with you?"

"Nothing," I said, and then, "Oh," as if I'd just remembered, "Can I hang with some friends tomorrow night?"

"Tomorrow? You haven't even watched any of the Guilds with me. You want to miss the *Oscars*? I already pressed your suit." This was true: Mom made me wear my communion clothes each year as we watched, she in a cocktail dress, and I'd caught her ironing it that very morning.

"It doesn't even fit anymore," I said.

She looked me up and down but clearly didn't want to make two short jokes in five minutes, so she left it at a glance. Instead she said, "What is this? Ragu again?"

"No. I mean, he'll be there, yes. It's just..." and we let the rest of my sentence hang there.

Finally she said, "I feel like I never see you anymore."

I looked at the air in front of my face, steam came off my breath like the smoke from her cigarette, and thought about breathing steam and smoke and air, and said, "I'm just going over in the late afternoon. I'm sure I'll be home for Best Picture. Those shows are endless."

"But what about Supporting Actor? They announce that first. What if he wins and you're not there?"

I felt pissed all over again. "Why is it so important?"

"I told you," she said, as we approached the car. "Because I never see you anymore."

"No," I said. "Why is the award so important? Why is *Tom Cruise* so important?"

She unlocked the car with a shrug and flicked her menthol into the parking lot, where it skipped into the snow. "Maybe your father will give me my money back if he wins," she said, and I said without thinking, "You'll have to find him first."

I didn't mean it. Or I meant it, but I didn't mean to *say* it. It was the first truly cruel thing I'd ever said to her, and she knew it. She looked like she'd been slapped. "Fine," she said quietly. "Go to your friend's house."

"This is gonna be sick!" Mallory said the next day, in Ragu's garage. She sat in a beanbag chair and slapped her knees, more energetic, less dreamy than I'd ever seen her at school. She wasn't wrong; I did feel sick.

"Big Man here bought it," Jeff Tansey said as he threw the baggie onto the table in the middle of us. "Inn'at right, Big Man?" he asked me. In front of Mallory, though, the tone he used when he said Big Man sounded deliberately ironic rather than complimentary.

"I didn't even know you did coke," Mallory said. "Since when?"

I looked at the clock. "Ten minutes from now."

She and Jeff Tansey laughed, and then she said, "So what's the deal? Your parents split and you started doing all this stuff to forget it?"

"No," I said, because that felt off. "It's not like that. It doesn't bother me that they split. I don't even think about it, really."

"Sounds like it's working then," Jeff Tansey said with an exhale of his Marlboro Red.

Ragu searched for a mirror.

"Why do we need a mirror?" I asked. It seemed a needless imitation of movie cokeheads to me.

"Why are you asking so many questions?" asked Jeff Tansey, and then to Ragu, "Why's he asking so many questions?"

Ragu ignored him, looked in a crate full of blankets. Lord knows why he thought there'd be a mirror under there. Instead Mallory answered, "Shut up, Jeffrey," to Jeff Tansey. Technically she was standing up for me. But the way she smiled at him when she said it, and the familiarity of *Jeffrey* made my stomach turn. I looked at the clock; Joan and Melissa Rivers were likely trolling the red carpet for fashion victims by now.

Ragu found his mirror. I expected everyone to take out razor blades or something, but they just casually ducked their heads down, inhaled, then shot back up, so I couldn't actually see anything ingested. When it got to me, Ragu poured out what looked like a miniature white anthill in an oblong circle. "Isn't—," I said, trying not to sound like a dork, "isn't it supposed to be in a line?"

"Not for a virgin," Ragu said. "Just a bump for you, to start you off man," and I took it. Everyone laughed. Ha ha, they went. But nothing felt funny anymore. It felt paradoxical, these people I'd known since kindergarten with bloodshot eyes and white powder under their noses, like one of Mallory's murals, those familiar cartoon figures distorted by alien contexts. Oddest of all, they just kept talking, like all of this was normal. "How's the car, Jeffrey?" Mallory asked.

"Badass," Jeff Tansey said.

"Tansey's fixing up a Dodge Charger," Ragu filled me in, before snorting a line of his own.

Jeff Tansey seemed irritated by the interruption and stared at Mallory. "I'll take you for a ride in it when it's all done. It's just like the one from *Fast Times at Ridgemont High*."

"The car in *Fast Times* is a Camaro," I said without thinking. Some substance dripped down my throat and I was having trouble moderating my thought filter.

"It's a Charger," he told me. "I know the guy whose car they used. For the real movie. He's a friend of mine, from Waldwick. And it's a Charger."

But my mind raced now and I couldn't make it stop. I didn't know anything about cars, but I knew about movies, and I needed something I knew about to feel grounded. "I don't know what to tell you. It was a Camaro."

Ragu, who also knew nothing about cars, said, "What even is a Charger?"

"It's like the General Lee from *Dukes of Hazzard*. It's a completely different car! This guy doesn't even know what he's talking about!" I couldn't tell how loud my voice was; I only heard it in my own skull rather than the acoustics of the room. But I tried to make my voice cartoonish to let them know I was joking and when Mallory laughed I kept going, "It's a muscle car!" I shouted, and flexed my nonexistent biceps, "A big, loud, angry muscle—"

The bottle exploded behind my head before any of us knew what happened. I looked at the wall where it had crashed, a Pollock-like splatter of Rolling Rock dripped down Ragu's garage. Jeff Tansey had missed my head by only a few inches, and by the time I turned back around, he was already popping the cap off of his next bottle. After a silence so pregnant it practically had triplets, he burst out in maniacal laughter. "You should see your faces!" he shouted.

"That was weird," Ragu said.

"I don't like being interrupted," Jeff Tansey said, though none of us could remember which of us, if any, had interrupted him.

I tried to wrap my head around the here-and-now of it all but I couldn't stop my thoughts. "*Fast Times*," I mumbled and then said it again and again, *Fast Times, Fast Times*, and my tongue vibrated on my teeth as I spoke so I said the whole thing, *FastTimesatRidgemontHighFastTimesatRidgemontHigh* and then a domino, *Fast Times* reminded me of Sean Penn reminded me of *TAPS* reminded me of Tom Cruise reminded me of Mom and I said, "I don't like this. I don't like this. How long does it last? I don't like this."

By now Jeff Tansey was on the beanbag chair where Mallory sat, nudged her over so that their legs pretzeled. He stroked her hair, whispered something in her ear that sounded like *little tin pans* but I couldn't make it out. I caught Mallory's eyeline but couldn't read it; she could have been as terrified of Jeff Tansey as I was or she could have been flattered by his attention or she could have just been miles off in her own coke-addled head. Who knows? I wasn't exactly a reliable narrator at this point. All I knew was that eyeline or not, she clearly wasn't looking at me.

I spotted the leash hanging from a rusty nail on the wall and something occurred to me that hadn't yet, in all the unpleasant baggage of the afternoon. "Hey Ragu, where's Jojo?"

Jojo was Ragu's German Shepherd, whom I hadn't seen since the last time I was over his house a few weeks ago and ached to see now, for comfort. She was a beautiful and friendly dog but also about three hundred years old and as soon as I remembered that, the room went thick.

"My dad is such an asshole," Ragu said. You have to understand that, outside of drugs and movies and music, Ragu wasn't exactly what you'd call a talker. I'd known him since kindergarten and those six words were until that point the most personal I'd ever heard him get.

"She was old. And she just kept shitting everywhere. It's my job to clean it up but I kept coming home late so he kept stepping in it. I mean she's a dog, you know? She couldn't help it. I told him it wasn't her fault, kick my ass if he wants someone to blame. But."

He was sitting on a milk crate, telling this story between puffs off a Winston, and left "but" in the air for someone to catch but no one did. Instead Mallory snapped out of whatever reverie she was in and said, "My stepdad thinks he owns our house. Walks around in these gross graying tighty whities all the time, right past my room. But ever since my dad died, my mom just wants anyone around who, like, qualifies."

Jeff Tansey had told me before we started that there'd be a lull after the initial bump and I assumed we were there. Everyone was just looking at the lonely, slack leash above the empty water bowl. Who knew whether Jeff Tansey even *had* parents, but even he had stopped stroking Mallory's hair and it felt like we were all thinking the kinds of thoughts I'd been wrestling with all weekend, all month, all year. Ragu said, "I wish Cliff Huxtable was my dad."

Mallory said, "Tom Hanks from *Sleepless in Seattle*."

"Tim the Tool Man Taylor," said Jeff Tansey.

"Tom Cruise," I said.

"When did he play a dad, movie man?" Mallory asked.

I thought hard for a second.

"He hasn't," I said.

WHEN I GOT HOME, all the lights were off—all except the glowing blue light from our TV. Mom was curled up on the couch, balled up tissues all around her, wearing her Oscar cocktail dress. She seemed asleep until I heard her sniffle, and I cleared my throat to let her know I was there.

She looked at me. Neither of us had any way of knowing what kind of night the other had had, but for a moment it felt like we did. "You ok?" I asked.

"Yes," she said, and without me having to ask the obvious question, she said, "He didn't win. But Michael Caine gave him a lovely shout out in his acceptance speech."

I nodded and sat next to her. I wish I could have told her then what I know now: that Tom Cruise and Nicole Kidman would themselves get divorced in just a few months. That it would be not Cruise but his ex-wife who would win the Oscar, just three years later—that she would ultimately be the agent of respect and accolades, completely on her own.

I didn't know any of that yet, though. I noticed the red light on the VCR and she said, "I taped it, just in case." She fired up the recording to the sounds of Billy Crystal's opening monologue while I put on my suit, pants and a button up that I was starting to outgrow, and soon, I knew, wouldn't fit me at all.

ELEGY FOR A SPORTING GOODS STORE

It wasn't difficult to get a job at Farrier's Sporting Goods. There were only two rules: you had to be a boy and you couldn't play sports. The first rule you could chalk up to old-fashioned sexism. The second one was practical: the jocks were at practice during the store's busiest hours, so they only hired non-athletes. The result of this was that the place employed a revolving door of teenage boys lacking the key formative entry point to the world of sports, namely: fathers. The kids who worked at Farrier's had them all: absentee fathers, deceased fathers, workaholic fathers, fathers who just didn't really give a shit. None of our dads had played catch with us in the backyard, let alone coached our little league teams, so none of us ever developed a taste for it. Bud was the owner and Billy the manager, and they took us in and taught us how to shave the scraggly hair on our teenage faces, how to tie our ties, how to throw our spirals, how to drive, how to change our tires once we got our licenses. They picked us up from jail after our DWIs and paid the fines when we couldn't. They bought us liquor to take to parties and drank a shot with us before we'd go, showed us how to down Johnnie Walker Red without cringing, just to prove we could do it. They gave us stacks of albums—AC/DC, Black Sabbath, the entirety of Led Zeppelin—and they'd quiz us on the details of, for instance, what city Ozzy Osbourne was in when he bit the head off a bat (Des Moines). Our cultural literacy came from their refusal to let us out into the world without this apparently vital knowledge.

They taught us about music and history and politics and TV, but their favorite subject, inevitably, was women. We'd get dumped and they were all too happy to weigh in, letting us know when we were feeling sorry for ourselves, when we were in the wrong, kept us from becoming resentful when our high school girlfriends cheated on us, commiserated with us when we didn't deserve it, made sure we took accountability when we did. Heartbreak after heartbreak, the boys of Farrier's would come in to work an afternoon shift, or a busy spring Saturday to fend off baseball and soccer and track season, and in between customers we'd toss around our sob stories while Bud and Billy shouted advice to us literally across the store so that all the customers would hear. No matter who we'd date, Bud would point out, "She ain't no Bethany Bellulavich," about our respective girl-friends. None of us knew who this person was, but Bud held her up as the end-all-be-all measuring stick against whom no woman could compare. Billy's advice was more practical. "She's geographically undesirable," he'd tell us if we dated someone who lived too far or too close. "Rich girls are trou-ble," he'd tell us when we dated outside our class. "Girls are more resilient," he'd say. "They're out there living their lives and we're stuck crying into our beers." We didn't question whether they were right. We scribbled down these idioms in notebooks like they were scripture, and if we didn't, we may as well have.

They had kids: Billy had two daughters and Bud had four. The store closed for a week during the Fourth of July each year and Billy saved up for twelve months annually to take his girls to Disney World. Bud's wife Dolores would drop his four girls at the store sometimes to run around and wreak havoc while she ran errands. Often, Bud would send us to his house as impromptu babysitters in a pinch. They were dedicated fathers, they lived for their girls, we could tell, but we also always got the sense that they liked this surrogate role with *us* they'd half been thrust into, half brought on themselves, in the land of fatherless sons and sonless fathers.

WHEN POLITICIANS TALK about small businesses, they're talking about Farrier's Sporting Goods. It was founded in 1964 by brothers Bruce and Arnold Farrier. The last name led to a lot of confusion when they first opened (even when I was working there, we'd get calls asking whether we sold horseshoes and equestrian gear). They opened it in a little strip mall that held a laundromat, a convenience store, and a deli, on the border of Midland Park, where I grew up, and Wyckoff, the wealthier town next door. In its first years it was the kind of mom-and-pop place that stapled suburban communities in the mid-twentieth century, low inventory, talkative guy behind the counter, fluorescent lights, neon orange price stickers, giant glass front window painted over by some local artist, wood panels, two hundred square feet total, if that. Word spread, the foot traffic fruitful, and soon all the middle and high schools in the surrounding areas were going there for their cleats and pads and helmets, the middle-aged parents going there for running shoes during their mid-life crises. By the 1980's, nearly every baseball, soccer, and football jersey in Bergen County's school districts was produced by Farrier's, ironing on vinyl letters and numbers by hand, one shirt at a time.

It was around this time when Bud bought the place. He'd worked there as a teenager in the 70's for extra bread after school. "I was so good," he'd tell us, "I could sell cleats to a baseball player!" ("Good," we'd say, "wasn't that your job?"). Bud was the first of our kind, a local boy brought in to man the register and fit kids for shoes and just generally make the customers feel tended to as the store's reputation grew. When he graduated high school he increased his hours at the store to afford tuition at Bergen Community College, where he studied business before dropping out when he realized Bruce and Arnold had aged out of their roles as store owners and sold the place to him, practically for nothing. "They almost paid *me* to take it," Bud would later tell us. "I should have known what a fuckin' headache the place was just from that."

CUSTOMERS WERE scarce by the time we worked there, in that sweet spot between the store's halcyon days and its waning last breaths. Bud was convinced the place would be overrun with customers at any minute, and so would have three or four of us work a shift at once, when one or none would have sufficed. He ran the place like air traffic control or the stock market, something high-stress, in need of constant surveillance, vulnerable to unpredictable chaos, rather than what it was, a hole-in-the-wall low-stakes corner store that sold jock straps to little league teams. We were poor kids from broken homes selling cleats to popular kids from rich homes and Bud knew it, which is maybe why he spent so much time motivating us. "Man your battle stations, boys!" he'd shout, to no one in particular. Billy told us that Bud watched George C. Scott's "Americans Love a Winner" speech from *Patton* every Saturday morning to ready himself for the onslaught of consumers (*consumptionists*, Bud called them, without apparent irony).

Still, megastores like Sports Authority picked off these consumptionists one by one, fewer and fewer of them popping in even to browse, mink-coated trophy moms preferring to drive their Mercedes' and Lexus' to the mall next to their Botox appointments, so we did what we could to keep ourselves busy. Bud had us do odd jobs for him, driving his wife to the airport, picking up groceries, bringing his girls to school sometimes. It was my job to pick up flowers and a card for his wife on her birthday ("A romantic card or a funny one?" I'd ask, and he'd say, "Surprise me"). One year I noticed he hadn't prompted me to pick up the annual flowers for their anniversary, a period when the store hadn't been doing well and she wasn't calling as much. Before school one day, I used my key to pop in and grab a hoodie from the rack since I'd left my jacket at my girlfriend's house. It was early, around 6. I was surprised to see the light on in the office. When I turned it off for whoever'd accidentally left it on the night before, I caught Bud sleeping on the couch back there, a suitcase of unfolded clothes open next to him like a slaughtered animal. He opened his eyes but only briefly, so that I wasn't sure whether he registered me. I came back after school for work and the suitcase was gone, as were his blanket and pillow. Bud was refreshed, alert, keyed up in jeans and a

KISS t-shirt. "You bring me my coffee?" was all he said when I came in.

THE STORE'S layout provided endless possibilities for bored teenagers with creative energy to burn, so we invented the Farrier Olympics. The glass bins in the middle of the show-room that held primary-colored Russell© sweatshirts became landing pads for racket balls we'd toss from across the store. We used the bench people sat on, discolored with age and cushions sunken in from suburban butts, as the net in impromptu games of tennis. The basement was its own gymnasium: six windowless aisles of unsold inventory, haphazard piles of boxes labeled not just with Nike and Adidas but also Umbro and Mizuno and BIKE and Shock Doctor and Mueller, vaguely categorized, divided by makeshift shelves. We'd turn off all the lights down there and attempt to tag each other with price guns in the pitch dark. We'd only come back upstairs if we heard the front door's bell ring, welcoming the rare customer, or if Billy got tired of covering for us and called us up the stairs.

Billy was forty, a once-promising minor league baseball star who'd shattered his knee, gotten black-out drunk, and woken up working there twenty years earlier. Where Bud was hyperbolic, cartoonish, insistent on maintaining some semblance of employee-boss relations, Billy spoke to us plainly, on our level, a friend or older brother. He'd roll his eyes at Bud's antics to make us laugh, but he'd also keep us in line when we fucked around too much. He took us all to *High Fidelity* when it came out, and for obvious reasons it resonated with us, Billy, going through a divorce at the time, possibly the most. It added another game to our unlimited list. "Top five three-piece bands," Billy'd say, and we'd utter the words *Nirvana* and *Cream* and *Rush*. Billy told us to get more cultured when we'd name Green Day and Blink 182; we accused him of being stuck in the 80s when he'd say The Police and ZZ Top, our arguments soundtracked by New York's Q104.3 Classic Rock station, which Bud kept dripping from the store's stereos at all hours of operation. DJ Carol Miller famously fought to make "Born to Run" our state's official anthem and Billy had a crush on her. We couldn't blame him. Anyone who felt that "A town full of losers, I'm pulling out of here to win" was a point of pride rather than a criticism understood us all deeply.

WHEN HE BOUGHT THE STORE, Bud had been half-right: he didn't really seem to need the doubtful rewards of an associate degree in business, since everything he needed to know he'd learned on the job. Bud knew everyone in town, a local boy made good: having been a popular party boy in high school, Bud turned those tenuous friendships into business by getting his old girlfriends to bring their sons in for Speed Demon© shin guards, their daughters in for STX© field hockey sticks. His old jock pals, the former star quarterbacks and varsity studs who were now alcoholic townies, coached Pop Warner and always bought the teams' merch from Bud. He hired Billy, then employed an endless line of teenaged dirtbags, probably in the hopes of molding one of us in his image, to his continued disappointment.

But it turned out Bud's hubris, like that of everyone from Greek heroes to the athletes we watched on the small screen in the store each day, was both his gift and his downfall. When the dotcom boom hit and the public rushed to buy their shit online, he dismissed it as a fad. He made small concessions to modernization. He began ordering sneakers with color in them, violating the place's decades-old policy of unflashy black-and-white thinking. He carried newer, trendier brands like UnderArmour, leaned in to the resurgence of Champion gear. He bought a credit card machine. This all proved, as you might imagine, too little too late.

We told him we'd help, we'd build him a website for people to order from, we'd happily box up shoes and cups and mouthguards and ship them out if that's what it took, but he resisted ("I know what I'm doin'. I been runnin' this store since you were swimmin' in your fathers' sacks," he'd tell us. Bud had a way with words). The internet was the one update he refused to cave to. Why he pushed back so hard, denied both the unsolicited help of a new generation and the foreboding signs of the demise of Mom and Pop, remained a mystery. All I knew was that the other boys who worked there came and left after a couple months, a hockey season at most, while I remained. Jeremy left for a job at a coffee shop, where most kids began to work in the early 00's as the Starbucksification of America took off. Nick went to school to study graphic design, offering one last time on his way out to use his new skills to build the place a website. Jimmy moved to the city when an old high school teacher of his stopped into the store and said,

"You *still* work here?" and he couldn't shake it off. Brian just stopped showing up, never told any of us why. But to the bitter end, something compelled me to keep going back every day, read magazines and play trivia games with Billy as the store became emptier and emptier, talk through my many heartbreaks with them, all the way to the day we packed the store up for good. I'd expected Billy to drive me home that final day, as he often did, but he needed to pick his daughters up and I ended up with Bud as my ride.

It was January, in the single digits, and we waited a few minutes for the heat to kick in, not saying much, just watching our visible breath fill the air in the car. I'd driven his truck countless times to the warehouse on inventory runs and knew it took forever to start up. We didn't talk about what he or Billy or I'd be moving on to next, whether he had another venture lined up. We didn't talk about what would happen to all the unsold stuff we'd spent the week packing up. We didn't talk about who'd be making the uniforms for the teams in the surrounding area from now on. We didn't talk about how his daughters or wife felt about the place closing. Or what business would move into the space next. Or retail's online future and the public's insatiable preference for convenience over loyalty, which he'd been talking about a lot lately. Or who'd teach me how to drive a stick shift, which both of them had promised they'd do. We didn't talk about the kids who'd worked there over the years or the way the place had become a club house for us, not even a home away from home because none of us really had homes anyway. Or the way we'd hang out there even on our days off, sometimes just to feel like there was a place we could go, where the door was open, where we had the key. We didn't talk about what compelled them to make it into a place like that, if they even did it consciously. Or what had compelled Bud himself to buy the store in the first place and keep it running past its sell-by date.

We didn't talk about Bud's first summer working there, which talked about a lot, renting a beach house in Seaside with some friends, driving an hour to work a shift at the store after not having slept all night, then closing up and driving an hour south again, a Miller in his hand for the ride, which he called the best summer of his life. We didn't talk about their daughters or my girlfriends over the years, or my mother or who or where my own father was. We didn't talk about Billy and Bud's friendship, how they felt about each other, which was always kind of hard for us to pinpoint. We didn't make plans, and didn't talk about when or where or even whether I'd see them again.

Instead we listened wordlessly to "Beth" by KISS trickle from his speakers. "I love this song," Bud said, to the dome light. I didn't love it—I thought Gene Simmons was an asshole—but it felt like it meant a lot to him in that moment, like whatever else he wanted to say had been expressed in those four words. So I just waited for him to put the car in drive. As he pulled away, I watched the store in the sideview mirror get smaller, then smaller, then gone.

FUTURE GIRL

When Molly Miller's brother died of AIDS her senior year of high school, she became convinced she could see the future. Her parents had split under the stress of his death and everyone assumed her belief was a sort of psychosis due to this wave of trauma, but she insisted it wasn't. She missed a month of school during which she didn't leave her house. Upon her return, our school let her miss whatever classes she wanted. Mrs. Miller, who'd always been kind of a hippy, brought her to a psychic. Mr. Miller encouraged her to focus her energy on college applications. He'd moved to Wyckoff, the next town over, and took Molly with him, on the grounds that it was a wealthier town and the school could afford a special grief counsellor to help convince Molly she was imagining things. We all felt bad for her so no one made jokes, not to her face anyway, but of course no one believed her either.

Except Andy. Andy Ryan had been her boyfriend since middle school and accepted her claims without judgment. I tried to do the same, but it was hard. She was telling me about how it worked, future-seeing, one night as the three of us sat in the Wyckoff Dairy Queen parking lot.

"Time isn't a line," she told me, drawing a line with her finger to demonstrate, "it doesn't have, like, a beginning, middle, and end. Yesterday didn't happen 'before' today. It just, you know, *happened*."

Andy nodded. I was a year behind them, a junior, and felt lucky to hang out with them. So I tried my best: "So it's next year right now?"

She shook her head, but warmly. She knew what she was saying was odd. "You're just applying the wrong prepositions to events. They don't happen in an order. Look at your clothes," she said, and pointed at them. "Did your shirt happen before your pants? Did your shoes happen before your socks? That's not the relationship they have to each other. They just exist at the same time."

I looked at my shirt. "I bought this yesterday," I said.

I was worried she'd think I was making fun of her, which I only kind of was. But she and Andy laughed. "You're a pisser," he said, and rubbed my head.

I'd borrowed my sister Emily's car to drive them around. This was a routine we'd gotten into: pick them up, ice cream, cruise down the highway, home. At first I'd been cautious to broach the subject of Future Girl. But eventually she'd volunteered the subject herself—"You can ask me, it's OK," —and since then it took up a lot of our discussions. "So, like," I said, "when exactly in the future are you from?"

Andy perked his head up, as though he wanted to know the answer to this himself but never thought to ask it. "It's tough to say," she said. "I can't tell whether I'm from the future or can just see it. I just have memories, except all of my memories haven't happened yet. Does that make sense?"

"Sure," said Andy. I was grateful for the save. "Are we still together?" he asked.

She wrapped her arms around his neck. "Of course. We're living in New York, in a loft. I'm an actress."

"A movie star," he said.

She shook her head. "Theater," which made sense—Molly'd always been the lead in the plays throughout high school, and read Ibsen and Inge and Pirandello in her spare time. "You're there too, Teddy," she said to me, though she was still looking into Andy's eyes. I felt flattered and almost asked what I was doing in the future until she said, "And the weird thing is, so's my brother."

ANDY'S DAD owned Ryan Auto Parts in town and Molly's parents were rich, from family money. This was partly why her parents never liked him, and they liked him even less when they found out he indulged her delusions. Mr. and Mrs. Ryan thought of the Millers as holier-than-thou muckety mucks and took the occasion of Molly's new reputation as Future Girl to forbid them from seeing each other anymore. That's where I came in. Andy failed English and ended up taking it again with the juniors, and when we got paired up for a class project we became fast friends. He was a popular if not-so-bright jock, great with cars and easy to get along with. But his friends, like everyone else, found Molly a little spooky and he couldn't drive his own car to her dad's house for obvious reasons, so when he found out I had access to wheels he roped me into being their unofficial chauffeur.

"You sound like you're their pet," Emily said to me the next day as I drove her to the train station. She'd moved back in with Mom and me after college a few months prior and took the PATH to Manhattan for her job in the city. It was my job to drive her to work, and I got to keep her car each day.

"I'm not their pet," I said. "I'm their friend. They're cool."

"Do they swing? Maybe they'll proposition you into a threeway," she said. She put her makeup on in the passenger mirror and I deliberately jerked the car to the right so she'd smear lipstick on her teeth.

"Can't I just like these people?"

"Like whoever you want. Just be careful."

"Careful of what?"

"I'm just looking out for you. You're prone to hero worship."

Ever since college, she'd been dropping terms like that all the time. Blasé. Bourgeoisie. Hero worship. Oedipal complexes. It was irritating, and I probably didn't help my case by saying, "You should see them together. I think they'll be together forever."

I kept watching the road but could hear her eyes roll when she said, "Christ."

"They will. She can—" I had the good sense to stop before I said *See the future*. Emily wasn't always like this— she'd made it all the way through college still dating her high school boyfriend, but he dumped her just before grad- uation and her plans to move across the country with him fell through, hence living back with me and Mom and hence too, I guess, her newfound cynicism.

Still, she was a lot smarter than me and I had concerns about my own possibly dangerous hero worship. So I said, "I guess it is a little weird."

"She's going through trauma," Emily said. I couldn't remember telling her about Molly's brother but I guess word travelled fast through town. "Andy's familiar. And it sounds like he loves her. And obviously they like that you're their biggest fan."

We were pulling up to the station but I didn't want to end the conversation just yet. We parked. She grabbed her stuff to get out and I thought, as I did each morning when I dropped her off, of our father, whom Mom dropped here so often with us in the car as kids. "Do you ever miss him?" I asked her.

She stood outside the car now, looking through her bag to make sure she had everything, her focus not really on me. "Huh? Who?" Satisfied she had what she needed, she zipped her bag, looked up at me and, in response to whatever face I was making, figured it out. "Not really—is this where you want to have this conversation? In the thirty seconds before I catch the train?" I shrugged. The whistle blew closer. But she relented. "Tell your buddies you're busy tomorrow night and we'll do something. Just the two of us."

EMILY and I had never been close. She was seven years older than me and in her last two years of high school—those years when Mom and Dad were throwing plates at each other's heads, when things got really bad—she'd basically moved in with Sean, her boyfriend at the time. They went to college together and lived there year-round, so she'd missed the fallout. I could see why she wouldn't miss Dad. Moving back in with Mom and me had clearly hit her as a defeat, her escape plan backfiring, and though she never talked about it I could tell she and Sean had had a messy breakup. She'd come home from work and go straight to her room and stay in there until morning. I don't know when she ate.

Her TV blasted Nick at Nite reruns in the deep sleep hours so I don't know when she slept, either.

But I'd been thinking a lot about her and Sean lately, not of their breakup but of the time I'd seen them together most, back when she was in high school. They'd been voted class couple in the yearbook. Mom and Dad had taken to sleeping separately by then, Mom in a sleeping bag on the floor in my room, so I tried not to go to bed until I absolutely had to. And occasionally Emily and Sean would take me to Blockbuster and we'd watch movies until late, me on the floor, the two of them sharing a blanket and throwing popcorn in each other's mouths to catch. Sean would ask me what I thought of the movies we'd watch. Emily would compliment my answers and say I was perceptive for a ten-year-old. I would have voted them class couple myself if anyone asked. And I thought of them a lot these days with Molly and Andy, feeling for the first time since then like a sidekick or a mascot or something, something this special unit of people actually wanted hanging around.

I was thinking about it that night as Andy and I drove to Molly's. "Everlong" by the Foo Fighters played from my sister's speakers—the acoustic version, which Andy insisted we play over and over whenever we drove around. I got the feeling he thought there were hidden messages in it.

"I really like the gold hat," Andy was saying. "I think I get it now." We'd finished *The Great Gatsby* in class the week before, but I suspected Andy hadn't gotten further than the epigraph: *Then wear the gold hat, if that will move her. If you can bounce high, bounce for her too, until she cry, "Lover! Gold-hatted, high-bouncing lover, I must have you!"* We were approaching Molly's dad's neighborhood in Wyckoff so he slumped down as always, to hide, but kept talking at a normal volume. "Do what you gotta do, right? Even if it's something stupid."

"I don't know that that's the point of *The Great Gatsby*," I said. "I mean, it's not this great love story or anything. He dies without Daisy ever fully loving him."

We pulled up to Molly's and there was an awkward silence in the car. I looked down at Andy, on the floor in the backseat, his shoulders slumped. "What?" I asked.

He looked at me, crestfallen. "He dies?"

"Sorry," I said. "Spoiler alert, I guess."

He looked at me through his fingers, smiling. "Guess I should've read past the title page."

We parked on a mountain in the Ramapo Valley Reservation, a spot that overlooked a lake soundtracked by crickets' and owls' chirps and hoots. Molly and Andy loved it from the first time I brought them. I was never outdoorsy but Dad took me there as a kid once, told me he went up there when he wanted to be alone, and had never shown anyone else the spot, not even Mom or Emily. I'd been there dozens of times over the years, brought girls to make out or groups of friends to do whip-its and shots. But Molly and Andy were different. They didn't drink or do drugs and they just liked the peace of the place. All they ever wanted to do was talk. That night, Molly told us to sit Indian-style in a circle. She brought a candle but it kept blowing out, so I turned the headlights on and they shone on us like a spotlight. "Do we need, like, a Ouija board or anything?" I asked.

She looked at me skeptically. "You wanted to know how it works," she said. "The future."

Andy and I were facing the headlights head on, Molly backlit by them, so all I could really see was her silhouette. Her brother had been a small guy, with a frame roughly the size of Molly's and a high-pitched voice, and the effect of her robbed of the features that distinguished the two of them spooked me. I wanted to be supportive, but I also wanted to be honest. "I have a hard time with this stuff," I told her. "I'm trying to buy into it but I guess I'm not there."

"OK," she said. "Let's try this. This is an exercise we used to do in my acting class. It's supposed to help you get out of your head." She picked something up off the ground and handed it to me. I couldn't see it until she'd put it in my hand: a shiny black rock, the size and shape of chewed-up gum. "What is that," she asked.

It felt like a trick question. "A rock."

"How do you know it's a rock?"

"Because I'm holding it," I said. "I'm looking at it."

"But how do you know what you're looking at and holding is a rock? How do you know what you call a rock is a rock?"

I looked to Andy for help. His eyes were closed and he nodded his head, like some tune we couldn't hear was playing through invisible headphones. I looked back down at the rock and said, to it instead of Molly, "Because that's what everyone calls it."

She leaned toward me and patted my knee. It startled me. "Exactly," she said. "A rock is just that which we call a rock, what we decided to call it. But what if you decided to call it something else? Does that make it something else?" For my only friend who didn't smoke pot, she sure talked like a stoner. I almost said that out loud but didn't need to, because it was like she read my mind when she said, "You think it's weird, it's OK. I thought it was too. Close your eyes."

The headlights gave her a little halo of fog in the aftermath of that evening's rain and I couldn't take looking at this rock anymore, so I complied. I did my best—she could deny it, but I knew Molly was going through stuff I didn't understand—and tried to let go of my skepticism as she spoke. *Clear your mind*, she said, but I opened one eye to look at them both; Andy still bobbed his head, eyes shut; Molly's face was a calm blank, like she'd already slipped into the deep meditation she now attempted to lull me into.

I closed both eyes again and tried. *You're not on this mountain*, she said, but I was of course—I could feel the ground beneath me and hear the crickets and owls, so I said, *Where am I then?* and she said, *You're not anywhere, you're everywhere and nowhere. There's no such thing as 'here,' what do you see—don't tell me, don't say it out loud, just communicate it to yourself in your head*, and I said *I thought I was supposed to be getting* out *of my head*, and she said *Shh, just tell yourself what you see*, but what I saw was myself sitting like an idiot, I couldn't stop picturing what I looked like, or what I'd look like to an outsider; I pictured Emily watching this and rolling her eyes and I couldn't not agree with her.

Molly stopped talking altogether. I looked at the Rorschach of weird light patterns that kaleidoscope in front of your eyes when you close them real tight. I didn't see anything until I opened my eyes. Andy and Molly were holding hands, looking at me.

"Molly was in a play," Andy said, responding to a question I hadn't heard asked. "Something old-timey, she had a corset on." She squeezed his hand and put her head on his shoulder.

It was my turn to talk next but I didn't know what to say. I hadn't seen the future and felt like a fraud. "See?" she said. "That's why I wanted to do this. You're special. I knew you'd get it."

 ～

"You know I knew her brother, right?" said Emily when she took me out the next night, for pizza. I should have known that—our town was tiny and everyone knew everyone, but the news took me by surprise anyway.

"What was he like?" I asked. I didn't want her to see my curiosity so I looked at my slice, patted it down with napkins to degrease it.

"Funny kid," she said. "Kinda goofy. Used to carry the *Village Voice* around with him everywhere. I thought it was weird at the time but in hindsight it was pretty cool." The TV behind her played a rerun of *Who's the Boss*. Mona said something about how fuckable Tony is and I let the sound of the canned audience cheering fill a beat. "How's Molly taking it?"

I winced, unsure how much to tell her. "She doesn't seem too bad, considering. She's told me some stuff that made it hard for her."

"Like?"

"She told me what he looked like at the end. Like a cadaver already."

"Jesus," she said. "She shouldn't be telling you things like that."

"Why not?" It seemed unfair that all I'd done was answer her question and she already objected.

"Because," she bit her stromboli. "You're a kid. You don't need to think about that stuff."

"I'm not a kid. I'm seventeen. I can drive."

"I wouldn't call what you do driving," she said, and I threw a balled-up napkin at her head.

I didn't want to switch topics yet, though. Emily could be a pain in the ass and she seemed depressed as hell lately, but she also had her feet on the ground. A lot of vague threads pulled at my brain lately, like a car radio stuck between two stations, the score for the ball game laid over a Zeppelin tune but too soft to hear either so you didn't know which teams or what song.

"Anyway," I started, carefully. "She says he's not dead."

She stopped mid-chew, wiped her mouth slowly, kept her eyes on me, like I myself was a ghost. "What are you talking about?"

I stirred my drink with my straw, stared at it as I talked. "She just has these visons of the fu—" I glanced at her horrified look and pushed forward as quickly as I could, "she has these visions of the future and she says her brother's part of them and don't worry," I held my palm up to her to stop her from interrupting, "don't worry, I know it's nuts and before you start psychoanalyzing, she knows it's weird too. I just…"

She looked at me, chewing, unblinking. It was just like Emily not to throw her two cents in exactly when I wanted her to fill the silence. I took a bite and pretended there was too much in my mouth to keep talking, but she didn't buy it. "It's just what?"

I shrugged.

"I don't respond to shrugging. I refuse to let my little brother become like all the other men I know. You obviously have something you want to talk about. Talk. Use your words."

I swallowed. "I've just been thinking that, like, is it so crazy, so impossible that someone can see the future or whatever? It feels…*wrong* to be so *certain* and just write it off. Isn't it at least possible?"

Her forehead scrunched, in contemplation or mock-contemplation, I wasn't sure which but was grateful either way. "You mean like chaos theory? Parallel universes? Alternate timelines? Quantum physics?"

"Sure," I said. I had absolutely no clue what she was talking about. All I'd meant was the gut feeling Molly had. But if there were credible schools of thought on this she'd picked up in college, I wasn't about to shoot it down. I lit a cigarette.

"You smoke too much," she said. Which was funny because actually I'd been cutting down since hanging out with Molly and Andy.

"I just mean people see their future all the time, right? They plan for their futures."

"Planning for it and seeing it isn't the same, bud."

"But it is sometimes, isn't it? Like, when people start a relationship, say. They plan on staying together for their whole future. And they can't *literally* see what the world will look like fifty years later, but they can work at it and make sure they're still together. They have control."

"Nobody has control of that. What are you talking about?"

Behind her head on the TV, Angela and Tony kissed, and the audience went wild with applause. "Nobody?" I asked.

Her face dropped, and I knew the look, like whatever private conversation she'd had with herself had been right all along. "See—this is what I was really worried about."

"What?"

"I didn't think you hanging out with Molly during her grieving process was inherently a bad idea. But I knew this is where your little mind would go. I knew *that* would somehow become about *this*." I took a drag to look casual but really I was nonplussed—another of Emily's favorite words. She waved the smoke out of her face. "You know what Dad said to me before he left? He told me you can't count on anybody. I was with Sean then and asked him whether another person can fulfill everything you need and he said, 'No. We expect too much of our partners. We expect too much of people in general because people are fickle and you can't count on them.'"

"That's what he said?"

"That's what he said."

"And then he peaced out on us."

She lifted her eyebrows. "You gotta hand it to Dad for teaching through demonstration."

I couldn't help but laugh. "You think he was right?"

"I think he was right that no one can fulfill everything you need, sure. But I think you can count on people to give you what they can, if they give a shit. I know what you're going through, kiddo. You're hitting the age where you realize that people let other people down. And it sucks."

I stubbed my cigarette in the ashtray and took out another one. "You're only twenty-three. Stop acting so world-weary."

She took the cigarette from my hand and placed it in her mouth, lit it with a match from the table, the Brother's Pizza label on the matchbox unchanged through all these years, one of the few constants I knew anymore. "Just be a normal kid while you still can. You only have a couple years left." I wished to God she hadn't said that.

SHE DROPPED me off at a party Gwendolyn Diaz was throwing. The party was OK, which is to say it was like most other parties I'd been to throughout school: a group of kids sat around a TV playing *Boy Meets World*, taking shots every time Mr. Feeny doled out advice; Gia DiPinto and Luke Morris broke up in the kitchen, over some infraction Luke had committed before I showed up; a senior girl chatted up a nervous sophomore guy on the couch while he peeled the label off his beer trying to figure out what to say; Frank Bosco did a keg stand in the back yard; bong smoke clouded the screened-in front porch; you could hear the ceiling creak and the muffled sound of two people having sex in one of the upstairs bedrooms; two guys in Grateful Dead t-shirts stared at the family dog and said, "What's he thinking? Can you hear it?"

I tried to do as Emily said: soak it in and be seventeen. But my heart wasn't in it, the crowd felt different. I was about to leave when I felt a hand on my shoulder, and turned around to see Andy.

"Hey," he said. "What are you doing here?" It had been a while since I'd seen Andy at a house party and it was weird, a foreign context, like when you see a teacher at a store in the mall. But he looked as at home here as he did every-where. I was the one feeling out of place.

I shrugged. "Emily dropped me off after dinner. She took the car."

He smiled. Andy had a great smile. It was like a gift he gave to certain people. He'd smiled at me the exact same way the day he decided to be my friend. "Let's go in the front yard, it's hard to hear in here."

He said Molly was at the library up the street, but that she was meeting him after, and then he asked what was wrong. I wasn't sure what he meant until I realized I'd lit a cigarette, even though I rarely smoked in front of him. "Nothing," I said. "Emily can just be a downer sometimes. It's my fault—I told her about Molly's, you know, future thing. And she as usual overintellectualized it. She doesn't think it's real."

I took a drag. The sound of the party inside swirled

around us. Luke and Gia made out now in the window. It wasn't until I blew out the smoke that I realized Andy hadn't responded, and when I looked at his face he wasn't smiling. "I mean," he said. "It's *not* real. You do know that, right?"

I thought I'd heard him wrong. "Huh?"

"Molly's thing about the future. You know it's just her going through stuff, right?"

I shook my head. "Wait—what the hell are you talking about? You said you saw it, too."

He held his palms up and said, "Well yeah. Her brother died. I'm trying to help her through it."

It had rained earlier and the muddy front lawn felt unstable beneath my feet, like quicksand. I shifted my weight to get my bearings but it wasn't working. "What about her being in that play?"

"What play?"

"You said the two of you were gonna live together. In a loft in the city. She was wearing old-timey clothes." I wasn't sure on the details but I knew I had them being together right, at least.

He nodded toward the street and without thinking I followed him, threw my cigarette at the house. The hill leading up to the library, which I'd walked a million times, felt suddenly insurmountable. "I've gotta take over my dad's shop when I graduate," he said. "And Molly's got too much going for her, I can't make her stay here with me. She hasn't told her parents, but she has an audition in Greenwich Village next week. She's taking the bus in. I guess we can't get you to drive us around forever." He laughed, but I couldn't see anything funny in what he said. Emily was probably right—I smoked too much, because halfway up the hill, in front of Eastern Christian Church, I ran out of breath. Andy patted my back as I coughed. "Easy, pal," he said.

I righted myself and asked, "So—are you breaking up? What's gonna happen next?"

He seemed confused by the question, as though I were asking who'd win the next World Series. "Who knows," he said.

I felt angry with him. With both of them. These people who'd made me drive them around, who'd adopted me, who'd tried so hard to convince me of unreasonable things —how was *Who knows* a good enough answer for them?

As though he'd heard the question, Andy said, "We love each other right now." We approached the library, where Molly stood at the front door waving, a stack of books in her hand. She was wearing Andy's football jersey, so large on her it looked like a muumuu. He lit up when he saw her. "You have to have a little faith in people," he said.

WE DIDN'T DO MUCH that night. We didn't talk about Molly's audition or acknowledge there was an impending goodbye, or that our drives together wouldn't last much longer. We didn't need to; it was in the air. Clouds from that day's rain remained in the air but were dispersing, moonlight breaking through like some werewolf movie. We walked to the graveyard at Nativity Church, where Molly's brother was buried, and sat next to his plot wordlessly. On the headstone, she placed a picture of the two of them when they were kids: Molly on a swing in a *Little Mermaid* bathing suit, her brother pushing her and laughing, a terrier I'd never met at their feet. Molly and Andy held hands, and she reached for mine.

"Thanks for coming," she said.

THE VIEW FROM HAWTHORNE HEIGHTS

Sandy Fisher's backpack had patches on it that said things like *Kill All Fascists* and *Parental Advisory: Explicit Lyrics*. She wore thrift-store jeans and Che Guevara t-shirts before they were mass-produced by Urban Outfitters a few years later. Her father was an adjunct history professor at Bergen Community College, the next town over, and her mother had died when she was a kid, I'm not sure how. She carried a copy of *A People's History of the United States* with her wherever she went. She was reading it one September morning in our Algebra II class, a class I'd flunked twice. Being a senior, I felt a little more confident about talking to girls now—if anyone rejected me I'd be out of here by spring anyway—so I turned to her and asked, "What's that about? The book?"

I thought she was annoyed at me for interrupting her, but it turned out she was just lost in whichever chapter she'd been reading. She smiled and tilted the cover up so I could see it. "Ever heard of it?"

"No," I said. "I'm reading..." What was there to say? "I've never seen anyone read a history book in their spare time."

"Well," she tried to explain. "It's a history book and it's not one. It's about how the history textbooks we usually read are trying to sell us a way of seeing the world that's imperialist."

I'd never heard of anything like that. Our school's text-books had fading covers and yellowed pages and taught history so dryly I couldn't get past one sentence, but I'd never thought that they were trying to make a point. They had end-of-chapter reader response questions that just asked about dates and people's names. Our teachers handed them to us about as unceremoniously as if they were blank stacks of printer paper.

"It's less pretentious than it sounds," she said, off of my blank expression.

"Hey," I said. "They're letting us leave at lunch to get food from anywhere we want in town. The seniors, I mean." This was a major privilege the school offered its upperclass-men: if you had a car, you didn't have to subject yourself to the school cafeteria's famously awful meals, months-old frozen pizza or slippery garlic pasta overcooked in vats of tap water. "I'm going downtown to pick something up. Want me to grab you something?" My lines didn't get much smoother back then.

"Sure," she said. "Can you get me a joint?"

I smiled. "You think you can sneak out to the parking lot fifth period? We can hotbox my car."

"Which one's your car?"

"The electric blue '93 Chevy Cavalier with the dent in the side."

She looked up from her book and batted her eyelids at me cartoonishly like an old-fashioned movie star, making fun of me, I think. "I feel like a princess," she said.

Ms. Doherty, our math teacher, stood up and I thought

she'd yell at us, but as usual, she just wrote *Ten Minutes Left* on the board, as though we couldn't just look at the clock. I couldn't remember what we were even supposed to be working on. Ms. Doherty had gone through a nasty and public divorce that summer and cared even less about the math lessons than we did.

When she sat back down, Sandy tapped me on the shoulder and said, "Hey, can my friend Caitlin come too? At lunch?"

"Caitlin Cilestro?" I asked, though there was no need to: the two were inseparable, and I knew asking Sandy meant Caitlin would be there too. I didn't mind. Caitlin was cool.

When Sandy said yes, *that* Caitlin, I said, "More the merrier. It's a beautiful September morning. It'll be a beautiful September afternoon."

And then Jon Lockhart popped his head into the classroom. Lockhart was one of those guys who isn't happy unless he's telling you something no one else knows, even if it turns out to be untrue: who cheated on who, which teacher just got fired, that kind of thing. He had that same anxious look on his face, like he had to pee, which meant he had something especially juicy.

"Hey," he said to the class. Ms. Doherty barely acknowledged the interruption. "A plane just flew into the Twin Towers."

I DIDN'T BELIEVE HIM, because a. it was Jon Lockhart, and b. the details were a bit fuzzy: a crash happened. One plane, maybe two. An accident, maybe not. I wrote it off as bullshit until I walked into second period, my film class, where the faculty tech guy, Mr. Esposito, sat watching a rabbit-eared box set with footage of chaos and a smoke-filled sky.

"Come on in," he said when he noticed our whole class waiting at the door, unsure of what to do.

The footage was surreal. Every channel played the moment the planes crashed on a loop, then haphazardly cut that with live coverage and commentary, so it was difficult to tell whether more buildings were getting demolished. The anchors narrated but weren't saying much, with nothing conclusive to report. It became clearer by the minute that this was no accident, if only because the odds were pretty low that two planes would crash by mistake in the same place on the same day only minutes apart, but everyone on TV was careful not to draw any conclusions.

When there was finally a lull in the onscreen discussion, Vinnie DePalma said, to no one in particular, "What do you think happened?"

The conversation didn't really come from anyone and we all seemed to be saying the same thing, one collective voice answering its own questions: *Probably got attacked. By who? Foreign country, obviously. No shit, which one? You know, that one. Which? The one that doesn't like us. No one on TV is saying it was an attack. No one has to, it's obvious. Let's not panic. Seriously? Nothing's for sure yet. Yeah, that's why I'm panicking.*

Etc. By the time the news came in that the Pentagon had been hit, around quarter to ten, we weren't even sure whether we were supposed to change classrooms when the bell rang for third period. Our principal, Mrs. Teraciano, must have been on the same page because she announced over the PA, "All students are to remain in their current classrooms until further notice. Please do not leave school grounds for any reason until instructed."

I had a weak moment: my gut reaction to this news was

only that I probably wouldn't be smoking in my car with the girls this afternoon. But that thought was interrupted when Mr. Esposito, almost despite himself, pointed out the window and said, "Look."

Our North Jersey town was only a George Washington Bridgeride away from Manhattan, and one of the, if not the, only things our school had to offer was that you could see the New York City skyline from certain angles of our football field. White puffs now clotted up the cloudless blue September sky that had beckoned to all of us the whole morning. It didn't take anyone long to realize we were looking at the aftermath of the Towers' collapse, which we'd watched in real time only a half hour before. We crowded the window to watch in silent wonder and then I heard my name being whisper-yelled from the classroom door.

It was Sandy, who'd snuck out of her classroom to find me. Esposito was distracted so I walked to her. "I don't think you're supposed to leave class," I said.

"I told them I had my period. Guy teachers don't ask questions when you tell them that, they just let you go for as long as you want. They're idiots."

"Smart," I said.

She looked over my shoulder at the window and pointed with her chin. "Pretty fucked up, huh?"

I shrugged. "No one knows what it is yet."

"I called my dad from the pay phones," she said. "He said he's worried."

"Why? You guys know someone who worked there?"

"No," she said. "He said this is what happens. People are gonna start hanging American flags everywhere and just doing whatever the president says. He said this is how we got into Vietnam."

"Fuck," I said, more for lack of an articulate response than out of frustration.

She shrugged and said, "Hey, does your dad still live in Hawthorne Heights?"

He did. My father moved out four years earlier into a condo a few towns over, the kind of bachelor-pad starter-home that men in midlife crises favor: hardwood floors, skylights, mirrored bedroom doors, a hot tub on the deck. The condo complex was called Hawthorne Heights because at its cul-de-saced peak you could stand at the dead end and overlook all of lower Manhattan, not just the skyline but the harbor and partway into midtown as well. I didn't see him much, but I'd thrown a few parties up there over the years and forgot until now that Sandy must have shown up at one or two, which is how she knew about it.

"He does," I told her.

She smiled and played with her hemp necklace, I hoped flirtatiously. "I thought so. I thought since lunch is a no-go, maybe whenever they let us out of here you could take us up there and we could look at the City. It must be a trip to see. Maybe tonight?"

I figured I could drive past his place to the top of the hill stealthily enough. Today of all days, no one was going to be paying close attention to anything but the TV. "Right on," I said. "You and Caitlin?"

"Caitlin can't come—her dad's a first responder and she's a little upset," she said. "But her boyfriend wants to come, is that OK?"

"Tommy? Why does he want to come?"

"I know he's kind of a rag, but Caitlin wants me and him to hang out more. We don't really see eye-to-eye on much."

It's not that he was a rag. It's that Caitlin's boyfriend was Tommy DeLuca. A senior, like me, Tommy and I grew up together but were never terribly close. He was an odd guy. He lived with his mother, a cashier at the A&P who walked with a cane, in a mobile home by the train tracks in town. It was hard to tell who his crowd was. You'd see him at parties every now and again, but he wasn't a mainstay anywhere; he wore army fatigues and combat boots but not ironically; he played bass in a friend of mine's band for about three weeks before quitting. During football season he'd shave his head into a mohawk and write the NY Giants logo in blue marker on his skull, but never seemed to mention the team in any conversation you ever had with him. As kids we'd some-times dare him to eat stuff—pebbles, dirt, dog hair—when we were bored, and he'd always do it, not because of a need to please us but rather because, it seemed, he didn't get why it was weird. But he grew nearly a foot over the summer going into senior year and a lot of the younger girls—Caitlin included, obviously—thought of him as the best-looking guy in our class (I'd overheard a few of them compare him to Heath Ledger at a party that August).

The other thing about Tommy was that his father was a Vietnam vet, an alcoholic who spent most nights doing shots of Old Crow by himself down at the town's VFW. Tommy had been fairly easily persuaded by the Army recruiter guys who hung out in our blue-collar town's strip mall, handing pamphlets to poor kids who needed a way to pay for their future. It wasn't difficult to imagine Sandy and him not having much to say to each other. But today it felt obvious what they'd talk about.

THEY DOVE right in when we got to the car that evening. Tommy sat in the passenger seat, fighting with the crappy flint on my lighter to spark the joint. Sandy lay across my entire back seat, flip-flopped feet dangling out the window, an old hoodie of mine under her head for a pillow.

"You think we'll go to war?" I asked, putting a piece of cardboard over the tape in the cassette player. It always jammed.

Sandy took the joint from Tommy and said, "Of course we will. That's our favorite thing to do in this country. Bush is a fucking fascist." But she said fass-ist, and I knew it was a new word for her to articulate, something she'd only until now read in the books her dad gave her.

"I *hope* we go to war," Tommy said, surprising no one. "I can't wait. I've been in basic training since the summer." The open window blew ash from the joint around the car, and Tommy wiped it off his camouflage cargo pants.

"You went to basic training during peace time," Sandy countered.

"Yeah," I said without thinking. "Aren't you at least a little freaked out," and then realizing how that sounded I added, "I mean—just, you know. 'Cause I would be."

Tommy shook his head. "Better than sitting at home on your ass."

Sandy shook her ass on the seat to pantomime it. "I disagree," she said. "No one ever got hurt by watching TV and minding their own business."

"Ever heard of Rwanda?" Tommy asked. "We didn't do shit but sit on our asses then. You know who got hurt? Almost a million people in a hundred days."

"Not all wars are good," Sandy said in a pinched voice, through an inhale. I wondered whether she didn't know about Tommy's dad. Then I wondered whether she knew about his dad but figured that since she had a dead mom, they cancelled each other out and gave her permission to talk to him like this.

"Not all wars are *bad*, either," Tommy said. "Sometimes there are things worth fighting for. If the cause is good."

"You think this is a good cause?" Sandy said.

"Getting back at the assholes who did this?" he said, and on 'this' he pointed at the white sky above our heads. "Yeah, I think that counts." He took a victory pull on the joint to emphasize the magnitude of his point, but she sat up and leaned forward.

"You don't even know who did it yet," she said. "You're saying 'these assholes' but you don't even know who you're referring to. You don't know whether it's a country or a militant group or some random psychos with too much time on their hands. It's just your go-to solution no matter what happened."

I have to admit that, despite the tragedy of the day, it was a little thrilling to listen to them. It wasn't exactly Buckley vs. Chomsky, but I'd never been part of a political argument until then, and hearing people my age make real points about something that mattered was something else.

Sandy rested her head on my seat, put her chin on my shoulder. Her hair smelled like hemp. She looked at my eyes in the rearview mirror and said, "What do you think?"

The tape I'd put in, "No Scrubs" by TLC, had finally begun working and circled the air in the car like the smoke from the joint. I took a puff and let out a laugh.

"Something funny?" Tommy asked like a Vice Principal in a quiet auditorium to a snickering kid.

"No, just...this song," I said. "It's so dumb. And this is what we're producing. I guess I've just been thinking that our generation feels so, like...undefined." Like I said, this was the first time I was talking like this and it was hard to find the right words. "Like, our parents had Vietnam," I looked at Tommy with as much respect as I could, "as you know. And their parents had World War II. And theirs had World War I. And we just have all this peace and prosperity, you know?"

Sandy lifted her chin from my shoulder and gave me a suspicious look. "So a generation is useless unless they go to war? That's very male of you."

"Not a *war*, necessarily," I said. "But something important. Like until now the biggest story of our lifetime was Clinton getting a blow job. And maybe what happened today...I mean, it's got us talking about stuff. That's something, you know?"

"And all it took was someone flying a plane into a building," Sandy said. She didn't say it mean. The conversation was heated but we weren't mad at each other. The pot helped with that.

"You always were a pistol," Tommy told Sandy, and she rubbed his hair and said, in her dad's voice, "Go to college when you get back from the army, big guy. You're smart."

At the base of Hawthorne Heights' long and winding road was a police barricade. Three officers stood cross-armed between the orange-and-white-striped barriers, and one poor guy who'd drawn the short straw directed the long line of traffic away from the hill.

"What the fuck?" I said as my car got closer. Tommy chucked the joint. I blasted the AC. Sandy sprayed perfume all over the car as we pulled up. We tried to keep straight faces.

An officer with a name tag that said *Brock* approached my window.

"Can't come up here," the guy said in a performatively gruff voice. "You wanna look at the City, go watch TV."

"But I live up there," I half-lied. "How do I get to my house?"

He didn't seem to believe me; I'm sure he'd been hearing that all day. "I.D.?" he said, holding out his hand.

I panicked for a second. My license had my mom's address back home on it, and I knew if I had to explain to him the complicated nature of my parents' divorce settlement, I'd sound stoned, which I was. I fumbled around and found an envelope with my father's address on it and matched the name to my I.D., which seemed to satisfy this Brock person, though he couldn't help adding, for our benefit, "Go on up. Motherfuckers have been coming by here all day, just to go up there and gawk. Like they're just sightseeing."

I had no idea how to react but Tommy held out his hand and sad, "I understand, officer. Thank you for your service." I caught Sandy rolling her eyes in the mirror.

Brock noticed the dog tags hanging from Tommy's neck. They were Tommy's father's, but Brock mistook him for a current recruit. Brock smiled, shook his hand, and said, "Thanks for yours, son." Tommy looked self-satisfied, his bloodshot, glassy eyes beaming, ready to mark this guy's respect down in the win column in he and Sandy's dispute.

Sandy, high, stuck her head out the back window and said, "Officer, settle an argument for us: are all wars good?" She began laughing before she could get the sentence out and Brock ignored her, barely able to contain his disdain. He looked back at Tommy and said, "Go get 'em kid. Go fuck those towelheads up."

Sandy stopped laughing. Tommy stopped grinning. The weird fusion of argument and camaraderie we'd had until then dried up almost instantly. The cops let me through and we were all quiet. I said, "Wonder if he smelled the weed."

No one wanted to talk. I turned the music back on, waited for TLC to drown out the silence, or maybe it was to linger while we still could in a moment when it was possible to listen to something mindless, which didn't seem so bad all of a sudden.

Tommy looked out the window and said, "Guys like that are fucking assholes."

WHEN WE REACHED THE TOP, the most alarming thing about the sight was that there was nothing to see: the city was invisible behind white clouds, but the lights from Manhattan shone behind it all and gave the whole scene a sort of ethereal graveyard glow. But the officers at the base of the hill had done their job: no one was at the top of Hawthorne Heights except the three of us. Tommy spoke first. "It's gonna be weird not seeing them anymore on the skyline. The Towers."

We nodded.

I passed out three cigarettes and we lit them, watched the smoke from our lungs blend with the smoke in the sky.

Sandy said, "Around here, everyone's gonna know someone..." She trailed off, but didn't have to finish the sentence. We knew what she meant.

RUMSPRINGA

Lately, Adam was becoming a problem.

He woke me up on my birthday and said, "Come outside." I checked my bedside clock.

"It's 5:30," I told him, but he was fully dressed, standing over me, with car keys jangling in his fist, so he must have been totally conscious of the time. "Where are we going?"

"I have a birthday surprise," he said. "I made coffee."

"That's not a good enough surprise to get me up at 5:30."

"The coffee is to wake you up. The surprise is outside."

"Outside?" I asked, but I was already stumbling out of bed, slipping on a hoodie and flip-flops. I'd known Adam since we were kids and I knew how futile it was to argue when he had a plan.

We slept on mattresses in our walk-up studio, two blocks from East Harlem, our sides of the room separated by a sheet, Greg-and-Marcia-Brady-style. It's all we could afford. Or all *I* could afford, anyway. Adam's father owned Reilly Plumbing, North Jersey's largest septic company, which Adam called the Shit Dynasty. He was destined to take it over once he turned 21. Adam worked constantly and had oodles of cash, all of which he put into our apartment. I could only imagine what he'd done this time.

I expected to come downstairs to the smell of brewing coffee, to have a few minutes to get my bearings, but Adam handed me a Styrofoam cup from the bagel place across the street. The words "birthday boy" were written on the side in magic marker. "I thought you said you made coffee."

"Made, bought. You have coffee. Come outside. Trust me, it'll be worth it," he said.

ADAM HAD ALWAYS BEEN AN ECCENTRIC. His high school bedroom in his parents' basement looked like a hipster's loft, a fifties beatnik paradise. When we were drinking stolen bottles from our parents' liquor cabinets, Adam was drinking coffee. When we smoked pot, Adam rolled his own cigarettes. When we threw parties in the woods, Adam drove into the city to talk his way into outdoor clubs. After graduation, the town emptied out. It was the kind of Jersey town Springsteen was always singing about. But Adam had to stay to learn the ropes of the Shit Dynasty—"It's my birthright as Poop Prince," he'd say, "I'm number two at the company"—and I couldn't afford school, so the two of us stayed behind and grew closer. Adam taught me how to line up trick shots in billiards; I designatedly drove us over the GWB. The only two people left in town splitting rent on a place seemed to me nothing more than a practical move, but as with everything else Adam did, he treated it like an adventure. He knocked on the doors of everyone in our building that first week and asked their favorite drink, then provided them a full bar with their names labeled on bottles at our housewarming. If I mentioned I liked seafood, he'd find a speakeasy that served sushi you wanted to propose to. If I mentioned I liked movies, he'd find independent film houses. He found hole-in-the-wall used bookstores, weekend street sales pawning black market goods only Manhattan could offer, and when it wasn't in Manhattan, we'd leave the city like there was no one holding us back, because no one was.

But then I got a late acceptance to Ramapo College on a scholarship, and Adam's behavior went from eccentric to erratic. He'd come home at four in the morning with an armoire and an oriental rug he bought from some guy in Connecticut and make me haul it upstairs with him. His road trips became less focused, more one-sided: he'd get a sudden urge to road trip to Syracuse or camp in the Catskills, always dragging me along. I don't know when he slept. He bought an easel and canvas and decided he was a painter—no, now he was a wine connoisseur, getting me drunk during tastings before I had to drive us back home. No, now he was a bass player, practicing the same Cure riff until daylight. And I would have put a stop to it. But I had an inkling what was behind it all, and was about to find out I was right.

"Happy birthday!" Adam said. We were looking at the back of an open U-Haul, at what he'd bought: a full-scale antique living room. Matching plaid sofa-and-love-seat set. Dialed TV complete with rabbit ears. Oak coffee table. And the coup-de-grace, leaning against the side, a stone slab pool table.

"It's from 1903!" he said proudly. "It turns 100 this year, and you turn 20."

"It's..." What was there to say? "It's stone. It must weigh 400 pounds at least."

"That's how they made them back then. We're going to have to caulk it if we want to shoot straight, but it'll be amazing once it's finished."

I wasn't sure where to begin. "Adam—how much did all this cost?"

"Don't worry about it. It's your gift. I just want to make the place nice."

"The place barely fits us with the stuff you've brought home already. Where are we putting it?"

I wished immediately that I hadn't asked the question. Adam pointed diagonally toward our building, just above our apartment, which was on the top floor. I looked back at those stone slabs and thought about our elevator-less building.

"The roof?" I said to the pool table, and he smiled. Like I said, Adam was becoming a problem.

ADAM WAS A BORN-AGAIN CHRISTIAN, but during high school, he'd exercised his family's faith in name only. We'd all get high together and ask him what Jesus would do and he'd say, "He wouldn't bogart that joint." During prom weekend he got hammered down the shore with the rest of us, but he woke up Sunday morning to visit whatever church was closest to the motel.

Lately, though, ever since my college acceptance arrived, I'd gotten the feeling his father was expecting Adam to adopt the family's zealotry as much as his role in the Shit Dynasty. As we'd grown closer as roommates, Adam had asked me if I wanted to attend one of his dad's sermons.

"Sermons?" I asked.

"Yeah," Adam said, shooting the eight ball into the corner. "He's a preacher."

I was confused. "I thought he ran the shit company."

"He does. This is just...an interest of his."

"Like stamp collecting," I said, but he didn't laugh. I knew why. Adam didn't invite anyone to his church. Our small town had all kinds of churches but Adam's stood out even among those. It was spooky. The entire building was the size of a Cape Cod. People called it the Fancy Hat Church because the women would file in in these giant, feathered hats straight out of a Flannery O'Connor story, six days a week. We couldn't figure out exactly what they believed in. I knew inviting me was a big deal. "Hey, sure. When's the next time he's—sermoning or whatever?"

THE TV WAS easy to get up the four flights of stairs. The coffee table took a little more work: we had to unscrew the legs and take it up piece by piece. By the time we brought the cushions up, it was 10 am and we needed a break. We sat on the cushions and Adam handed me a Corona.

"Thanks," I said, annoyed, popping off the cap. "How the fuck we getting the rest of it up here?"

He walked to the edge of the roof, looked down at the U-Haul. "Initiative."

"Great," I said, and checked my watch. "You think we'll be done by two?"

He rectangled his hands and closed one eye, like a director getting the right angle. "You know, I bet we could pull the love seat up the side of the building. I'll run to the store for some rope..."

"Adam—"

"...and the sofa, we can pivot it through the thresholds and get it up here, no problem."

I threw my bottle cap at his head but missed, and it went sailing over the side. "I'm supposed to meet Kayla. She wanted to take me out."

That got his attention. "The girl from the train?"

I'd met Kayla at orientation. She was a pretty girl, the first I'd ever met who I hadn't grown up with. We'd scheduled some classes together and taken the train home to Grand Central. Every question she asked signaled my new life, away from my hometown. "Yeah," I said. "That one."

He pushed the lime through the neck of his beer and walked to the unplugged TV, fidgeted with the antennae as though he were trying to get a clearer picture. "Tell her to come here. By then, we'll have this all set up. It'll look great. A birthday party for three. I'll make burgers."

"She's a vegetarian," I told him, but he was already escaping down the fire exit.

WHEN I'D SHOWN UP, Adam's church looked bigger on the inside than the modest exterior suggested. It reminded me of the establishing shots in *Friends*, when the actual crowded New York buildings never quite matched the lavish space of Monica and Rachel's. I'd shown up alone, in a tie but no jacket, just to make sure no one thought I was actually taking this seriously. The people spoke to each other like neighbors, which was weird because none of them were from our town. I hadn't been in a church since I was a kid and couldn't hide my discomfort. Every inch I moved felt blasphemous. I kept telling myself not to think about sex and then pictured priests fucking nuns reverse-cowgirl style. But I liked the camaraderie of the place at least. Everyone smiled at me as they entered the pews.

When Adam's father came out, the crowd shut up. It felt so theatrical I expected them to applaud, for the pit to strike up the overture. He walked to the podium, Adam following behind, head bowed, a miniature version of his dad dressed in an identical suit, like a ventriloquist's dummy.

"I want to talk today about forgiveness," Adam's dad said. No other lead-in. Just that. He looked at Adam. "You all know my son. He's been part of this parish since he was born. He'll be up here talking one day." The congregation murmured approval but quieted down when he spoke again. Adam's dad wasn't the kind of guy you wanted to disobey. "My son is part of a generation I've been thinking a lot about lately. A generation maybe you've all been thinking about, too. I know some of you have kids his age. He's a good kid. The influences around him, though..." he patted his forehead with a handkerchief, and I almost laughed. It was like a pantomime of a televangelist, what you'd do if you wanted someone to guess "preacher" in charades. I looked at Adam to make him laugh, but he was looking at the ground.

"My son is going to face some hard choices in his next few years. It's tempting to see the world. To leave your family, your responsibilities, your church. It's tempting to follow the path your friends go down." I blushed. I wasn't sure whether Adam's dad knew I was coming that night but it sure felt like it. College was on the horizon. Things were looking up. Adam's dad placed a hand on Adam's shoulder while looking at the crowd. "But what we need to remember is, for whatever their transgressions, we need to embrace our children. To bring them back to the light. To practice forgiveness. In the name of the Father..." he finished. He and Adam hugged.

I wanted to punch his father for embarrassing me, even if no one there knew who I was. I wanted to hit him for talking about his own son like he wasn't in the room. And then I wondered whether Adam knew about tonight's sermon, whether there was a message in there he wanted me to hear.

BY NOON, we'd gotten the sofa to the top and I was ready to kill him. Our neighbors had caught on to what we were doing and gathered in front of the building to watch as we hooked up Adam's makeshift pulley to the love seat. It fell right away on our first attempt. On the second, it was halfway up before it fell crashing to the ground. "It's salvage-able!" our downstairs neighbor Suzanne shouted after inspecting it, and our neighbors cheered. They strapped it up again for us, and this time we got it all the way to the edge of the roof, grabbed both ends, and pulled it over.

Adam lifted my hand over his head like a prizefighter and the crowd went wild. I wanted to feel triumphant, but I looked up at my watch and winced. "Shit. It's almost two."

"The pool table," he said, like I'd left the dinner table eating hors d'oeuvres but not the steak.

"That'll take hours. Days," I said and he said, "*An* hour, tops," and I told him, "We're gonna have to bring each piece up floor by floor and stop at the top of each stairway," but he wasn't having it: "Just tell her to come later."

"I have to shower. I can't have a girl over like this, I reek."

He turned, shouted down to our neighbors, "He doesn't think we can get the pool table up!"

"Boo!" they shouted. "Last piece!" "Birthday bitch!" "Pool table! Pool table! Pool table!"

He looked at me, took a swig of his fourth Corona. I wanted to push him off that ledge. I called Kayla and told her to come over that evening. She agreed. "Let's go, asshole," I told him.

ADAM HAD BEEN the one to find the place. When I suggested we live together, he became obsessive about it. He'd call me with ten places a day. We'd drive past them after we were both off work. Since we both worked in Jersey, I asked why he was so set on a place in Manhattan.

"Rumspringa," he told me.

"Isn't that for Amish people?"

"Ceremonially, yes. Self-imposed, no."

"You're enacting your own personal Rumspringa? Because what, after a year you have to take over your father's business? Sounds good to me," I said.

"Sure," he said back darkly.

I don't think I'd picked up on the tone of his voice until we had the final stone slab on the fire escape. "Adam," I said, under the weight. My arms felt like rubber bands by now, my fingers raw.

"One more push!" he shouted at me. He was on the roof, pulling it up, and his face was purple. I was afraid he'd pass out and the slab would fall on me. But somehow we got it over. The crowd had dissipated, so there was no one to cheer us on, and whatever satisfaction I'd hoped to feel from finishing didn't come. I just looked at the ground, pissed. We lay there beaten, sweaty, as though we'd just been in a fist-fight, which is probably why I said: "You're a dick."

I placed a beer from the cooler on my forehead. When the words came out I recognized how much I meant them in that moment. My 20th birthday had been taken from me by yet another one of Adam's stupid impulsive schemes disguised as being for my benefit. "Did you hear me?" I asked. Adam didn't say anything. He just lay there like he was about to make a snow angel.

"Whatever," I said. "I'm showering."

It took me longer than usual to get ready so I was grateful that Kayla was late. I didn't want to have to talk to Adam and I wanted to look good for her, so I spent an hour in the bathroom. Kayla knocked on the door just as I was getting out. She looked—collegiate. I was psyched.

"What took so long?" I asked her, and she looked at me and said, "You're kidding, right? I've been waiting all day," and blood rushed to my face. "What took *you* so long," she asked, and since the beers were still in the cooler on the roof, I figured I'd bring her up there, take her out of my cramped shithole apartment to show her the dilapidated junkyard we'd turned the roof into.

Only when we got up there, the roof wasn't the roof anymore. Not the one I'd left an hour ago. The furniture was set up as neatly as a homey living room, way more comfy than any room in the house I'd grown up in. Adam had strung white Christmas lights along the roof's edges and set up tiki torches in all four corners. He'd used an extension cord to hook up the TV and a stereo. And there he was, flipping burgers—two beef, one veggie patty—on a grill next to the stone slabs.

"This is amazing," Kayla said. Adam turned around and they introduced themselves.

I sat on the couch, speechless. "You're going to Ramapo, too?" Adam asked Kayla.

"Yup. Planning to move to Boston when I'm done. Or I have a friend in Dublin who wants me to live with her after I graduate. Ramapo has a great Communications program."

He handed her the veggie patty and said, "That sounds nice for you," and then handed me mine and said, "Both of you."

I poured all three of us beers and said, "Next year," but trailed off. It suddenly occurred to me that Adam wouldn't be here next year. Or the years after.

"Happy birthday," he said, taking his glass from me, and Kayla said, "New friends," and raised hers. We played beer pong by the firelight. We danced to the new Strokes album. We jumped on the couches. We did the things you do when your life is starting, and when it got too late, Kayla and I went to bed, but Adam stayed up there all night, sleeping under the stars.

IF I CALL YOU UNCOUTH

In June, Meg takes me to get matching tattoos. This is the summer after our freshman year of college. We'd planned to get them right after graduation, but prepping for college got in the way. We're drinking wine coolers in the 7-11 parking lot afterwards and I start picking at my bandage.

"Stings," I say. "Hurts like a bitch."

She takes a pull from her bottle and says, "Only hurts like a bitch if you act like one."

"You're drinking Zima. You can't pull off grizzled comebacks."

She sticks her tongue out at me. I scratch my arm. "Don't," she says. "You'll infect it."

"It itches," I say. Not exactly. It feels like a sunburn contained to a three-inch patch of my bicep.

"Just lightly slap it," she says, and demonstrates on her own arm. I do the same and it works.

"How'd you know to do that?"

She lifts her tank top to show the Chinese symbols lettering her rib cage, thick and black and exotic-looking.

Without thinking or asking, I touch it. "When'd you get that?"

"My roommate and I went."

What did we just do then, I want to ask. What kind of a memory are we making? I am the Buzz Aldrin of friends, I'm thinking. But I don't dwell on it. This past year has rained shit and I'm grateful to have my friend back. "What does it say," I ask.

"It's supposed to say 'serenity' but some kid on my floor told me it says 'sandwich.'"

"Serenity's stupid too," I say. I finger the ink on her side and she lets me.

I reach for another bottle, pop off the top. "Slow down on that, we've got a whole night ahead of us," she says, and reaches into the backseat of her car for something.

"We were kids once, you and me," I say, but she doesn't hear it. It doesn't make sense anyway. She leans back out with her camera in hand. Meg is a photography major at Syracuse's Newhouse program, number two in the country for photojournalism. I'm commuting to community college where they don't make anyone declare majors, they're just happy if you show up.

She snaps a photo of me with the bottle to my lips. "Do that again. I need to catch the light."

"Do what? Who cares about the light?"

"Lighting is everything," she says, but the words sound aped, like she's sounding them out to make sure she's got the phrasing right. "I'll make this into a series. I'll call it 'College Aged Punk in a Prepubescent Body.'"

I give her the finger and she snaps another one. "That'll be the cover shot," she says.

∽

MEG and I have known each other since we were born. Literally. We share a birthday and our mothers were in Valley Hospital together. We grew up on Vreeland Ave, four houses apart. Meg's were the first boobs I ever saw, though they weren't boobs yet; we were in first grade and in bathing suits in her garage and she was showing me what she had under there and I was showing her what I had under mine, and we eventually stopped flashing each other and just stood there naked, staring, until her mother walked in and told us to get dressed. Her mom made us BLTs and when my mom picked me up our mothers looked at each other like *What have we gotten ourselves into* and then my mom took me home and never mentioned it again.

When Meg and I were in sixth grade we sat next to each other in every class. When my parents divorced that year no one talked to me except the other divorce kids and Meg. Neil Carius asked her to the Valentine's Day dance and when he ditched her for Gia DiPinto the night before, I egged his house while she stood on the sidewalk and laughed. In eighth grade I stole a bottle of Vermouth from my mom and drank the whole thing at a party—Meg snuck me into her house and called my mom to say I was sick, and I spent the night puking into her toilet. In high school we could no longer sit next to each other because Meg was placed in the honors courses and I was too high and skipped too many classes to qualify, plus I wasn't smart. I starred in her honors English capstone video on *Beloved*. She finished all of my algebra homework, blew through it like it was times tables. I brought her to the late-night keggers my friends threw in the woods. She helped me hook up with the straight-A girls in her class who were way out of my league.

When Lindsay Adams broke my heart senior year, Meg drove me around town to distract me, down the lampless, legendarily haunted Clinton Road and told me she was a vampire, laughed her head off when I got spooked. When Meg's dad took OxyContin after a shift at the A&P, she'd sneak in my window and we'd stay up all night talking about teachers and kids we hated, and movies and sex and politics, anything except for parents. She drove me to school every day. I bought her first pregnancy test so no one working the register in our small town would see. We were dating other people senior year but my girlfriend and her boyfriend didn't bat an eyelash when Meg and I went to the prom together. We called each other "estrogen twin" and "testosterone clone" because we felt we were the negative-print gender versions of each other, hence our tattoos of the Gemini twins, a couple of idiot brothers who Zeus made immortal in the stars.

SHE TELLS me she has a surprise. We walk up Vreeland from the 7-11 and toward the high school.

"Is the surprise that you're making me go back to the high school? I hate that fucking place."

"It'll be fun. Try and keep up." I'm walking a little crooked thanks to the alcohol. I've switched to whiskey now that the night's under way. We're quiet long enough for me to wonder what Meg sees when she looks at this town, now that she's been away for a year. What does this girl, whose mother complains to me weekly that her daughter doesn't answer phone calls, think when she returns to the land of the townies?

"Hey, seriously, ease up on that stuff," she tells me as I swig. "It thins out your blood. That tattoo's gonna look like the elevator from *The Shining*."

As we get closer to the high school I hear the horn section floating in the air from the football field and I remember tonight's the Pops Concert. It's this stupid thing where they let the seniors perform whatever they want: songs, skits, guitar solos, anything under six minutes. I always found it obnoxious, giving the theater kids a show-case to jerk themselves off, but Meg loves it.

"So you finally got me to go to one of these," I say when we get there. We're sitting on the hill near the tennis courts, far enough away from the bleachers that no one will small talk us. We pass the bottle as a pair of girls sings "Bosom Buddies" from *Mame.* Everyone is wearing black: black button-ups, black slacks, black sundresses, black character shoes, black berets in their hair. It feels like a eulogy.

"Remember when we spent the whole night drinking with socks on our hands?" she says when she almost drops the bottle. "You thought I'd piss my pants."

I scrunch my nose. "We never did that."

"Surrre," she says. "Whenever I win a bet, it gets lost to the annals of history." I take out a cigarette, try to conjure up whatever she's talking about but nothing comes. I light it and shrug.

"Do you seriously not remember this?" she asks. The *Mame* girls finish and up comes a kid with shoulder-length surfer hair and a guitar who I'm unsurprised sings "Crash" by Dave Matthews. Meg stares at me in shock before her face falls and she goes, "Fuck. You're right. That was Seth."

"Friend from Syracuse?"

"Kayla's boyfriend," she says. I have no idea who Kayla is. I offer her a puff of my cigarette and she waves me off. "I quit," she tells me. "Have you ever tried hookah?"

"Around here we aren't quite that worldly yet. We're into this new exotic drug called 'coke'," I tell her but she doesn't laugh, just watches Dave Matthews boy belt out flat notes. She's savoring it, the way you concentrate on every bite of a meal from a restaurant that's going out of business.

She's about to say something that starts with "I've always..." but before she can finish, her phone buzzes. She blushes when she sees who it is and looks at me with big eyes. "Sorry. Gimme a sec." She stands up and holds the phone to her ear. "Kayla!" she says in a voice I've never heard before. She sounds like my mom when she's entertaining guests and acting like we aren't poor. She sounds like me when I'm drunk and trying to convince people I'm ok to drive.

I'm about to lift the bandage off again when Charlie Matz walks past. "What's on your arm?" he asks. Charlie drives trucks for the company his dad has worked at since we were kids. He barely got a diploma and wasn't allowed to walk with us at graduation. He tells me there's a party in someone's basement tonight, which there always is, and I tell him I have other plans.

He laughs like I just told him I bought a pet octopus: "What other plans do *you* have?" Meg walks back over right on cue and Charlie goes, "No shit! The college broad! What's crackin'?"

"Hey Charlie," she says and gives him a hug.

He takes out a cigarette for her and I say, "She quit." I can't keep the contempt out of my voice.

"I was just tellin' this asshole there's a shindig downtown if y'all feel like joining us. Though I understand if these theater kids are more entertaining." He points a thumb over his shoulder at the kids onstage now, asking the crowd suggestions of "place" for their *Mad Libs*-style improv.

"I'm actually," Meg says and I say, "We could," at the same time so she says, "Sorry," and I say, "No you go," and she tells Charlie, and me too I guess, "A friend of mine from school lives a half hour south. She wants me to head down tonight, stay for the weekend." I can't tell whether this is her making up an excuse not to join him or real plans she's made to bail on our night. I look at Charlie and then at Meg and then at him and then at the stage and then at Meg again. She looks at me like *You can go if you want to* and I look at her and shrug *Do you want me to go* and she squints *I'm not your boss* and I raise my eyebrows *Would you even want to go to a party like that anymore* and she looks at her shoes and raises her eyes to me *Don't talk to me like that*, and we're good at conversations like this, eye dialogue. Charlie's just watching us, his eyeballs ping-ponging back and forth as some sort of understanding passes between us. Her phone buzzes again, and for once, I can't read her expression.

IN THE FALL Meg will go back to Syracuse and rejoin her new friends in her new life at Newhouse. She will score an internship over winter break for *National Geographic* and won't come back for Christmas. She'll begin dating a WASP named Charles from Connecticut who comes from old money, whose family has a yacht named Rover and an Irish setter named the SS Minnow. She'll gain a reputation among the faculty as a sporadic worker but an undeniable creative; they'll value her for her keen eye and bohemian sensibility. They'll compliment her on funneling her working class roots into her work, she'll regale them with stories of her charmingly scrappy upbringing at cocktail parties at the Getty. She'll be a campus celebrity before her junior year.

I'll sleep my way through the townies and when they leave, I'll start sleeping my way through the senior girls who haven't glimpsed the future yet and still think I'm something. I'll work at the sporting goods store I've been working at since ninth grade and fit more successful classmates' little brothers for soccer cleats. I'll live at my mom's house even after I have enough for an apartment because she doesn't have anyone to take care of her. Bergen Community won't do much for me but my grades will be fine. And then, after a few semesters of sleepwalking, I'll land in front of one of those teachers who actually gives a shit, and I'll start to care.

Two years from now, when she's a junior, Meg's uncle will kill himself. Her family will tell the world it was an accident. I'll be the only one who knows. Meg will fall into a depression she can't name. She'll hit the denial stage of grief and just linger there, she'll shut off her parents and her hometown and me more than she already has. She'll shut out her school friends and her internship training and her classes, too.

The funeral will be weird. I'll wear a gray suit because I don't own a black one and can't afford anything new. I'll chain smoke in the parking lot with her father, who won't know how to talk to the women in his family. He'll be high. He's always high. Meg will drink too much at the after-party thing and her mom will ask me to take her home.

We won't talk in the car. We won't have talked for months by then. I'll blame that on the tragedy but the truth is that it's we ourselves who'll be responsible. We ourselves will stop trying. I'll transfer to Ramapo on a writing scholarship by then and will apply to graduate schools in Maine, Oregon, Arizona, anywhere that isn't my hometown. Meg will drop out of Syracuse and move back in with her parents. She'll meet a townie who graduated with her older sister. He'll work at the local lumberyard and be missing four fingers. But he'll be kind and to her it will feel like the first time anyone has been kind to her in ages and she'll marry him. I'll become a professor wherever I get my MFA. Meg will buy the house next to the one she grew up in. Or I'll assume she has—by then, we'll have lost each other's numbers. It takes effort not to put in effort.

But I don't know any of that yet. Right now we're just watching the two sisters on stage sing the harmony from "Power of Two" by the Indigo Girls. It's a difficult song and we're both impressed.

"Damn," I say. "Little bastards can sing. Who knew?"

I look over at her and she's holding the camera up, aiming the lens at me like the scope on a gun. She snaps it. "You know what that is?"

"What?" I ask, because I don't know what she means.

"That's you letting your guard down for a second," she says. "That's the kid I love." I can't remember the last time someone called either of us "kids." Her phone buzzes again.

"You can pick that up if you want," I say, and she shakes her head and purses her lips. "She can wait," she says, and adds, "You can go to that party if you want," and I shake mine and say, "They can wait, too." We lie back on our elbows and just at the foot of the hill I catch sight of two middle-schoolers, a boy and girl, chasing fireflies. "Think they'll catch any?" I ask Meg.

"They're not chasing fireflies," she says. "They're chasing each other." She's right. Maybe it's tag. He must be 'it', because he keeps sprinting toward her and reaching out his hand but she's just out of reach. But he keeps trying and she keeps letting him, like they have all the time in the world to catch up to each other, like they're gonna be on this field forever.

I rub my arm. "Still stings," I say, slapping the bandage.

"Don't worry," she says, to me obviously, though she keeps looking at the kids. "The pain will go away. After a while, you'll forget what even caused it, you'll forget it's even there."

PUBLICATION CREDITS

- "Cicadas" first appeared in *Los Angeles Review*, 2021
- "The Goddam King of the American Dream" first appeared in *Reed Magazine*, 2023
- "The Freaks Who Suspect They Could Never Love Anyone" first appeared in *Ninth Letter*, 2022
- "Elegy for a Sporting Goods Store" first appeared in *Cumberland River Review*, 2024
- "Future Girl" first appeared in *Glassworks*, 2023
- "The View from Hawthorne Heights" first appeared in *Hash*, 2022
- "Rumspringa" first appeared in *Passengers*, 2021
- "If I Call You Uncouth" first appeared in *Juxtaprose*, 2020

ABOUT THE AUTHOR

Ted McLoof teaches English and Creative Writing at the University of Arizona, but he is and always will be deeply from New Jersey. His work has appeared in the *Los Angeles Review, Kenyon Review, DIAGRAM, Hobart, Minnesota Review, Ninth Letter, The Rumpus,* and elsewhere. His story collection *Anhedonia* was published by Finishing Line Press in 2022. *Empty Calories and Male Curiosity: Stories* is his second book.

www.ingramcontent.com/pod-product-compliance
Lightning Source LLC
Chambersburg PA
CBHW031057310726
48969CB00007B/2313